How About No

Book 3 of The Bear Bottom Guardians MC

By

Lani Lynn Vale

Lani Lynn Vale

Copyright © 2018 Lani Lynn Vale

All rights reserved.

ISBN: 9781730938894

Dedication

To cold and flu medicine. You make life somewhat worth living during days 2 and 3 of a cold.

Acknowledgements

Golden Czermak- Photographer

Danielle Palumbo- My awesome content editor.

Ellie McLove & Ink It Out Editing- My editors

Cover Me Darling- Cover Artist

My mom- Thank you for reading this book eight million two hundred times.

Cheryl, Kendra, Diane, Leah, Kathy, Mindy, Barbara & Amanda— I don't know what I would do without y'all. Thank you, my lovely betas, for loving my books as much as I do.

CONTENTS

Prologue
Prologue II
Chapter 1
Chapter 2
Chapter 3
Chapter 4
Chapter 5
Chapter 6
Chapter 7
Chapter 8
Chapter 9
Chapter 10
Chapter 11
Chapter 12
Chapter 13
Chapter 14
Chapter 15
Chapter 16
Chapter 17
Chapter 18
Chapter 19
Chapter 20
Chapter 21
Chapter 22
Chapter 23
Epilogue

Other titles by Lani Lynn Vale:

The Freebirds
Boomtown

Highway Don't Care

Another One Bites the Dust

Last Day of My Life

Texas Tornado

I Don't Dance

The Heroes of The Dixie Wardens MC
Lights To My Siren

Halligan To My Axe

Kevlar To My Vest

Keys To My Cuffs

Life To My Flight

Charge To My Line

Counter To My Intelligence

Right To My Wrong

Code 11- KPD SWAT
Center Mass

Double Tap

Bang Switch

Execution Style

Charlie Foxtrot

Kill Shot

Coup De Grace

The Uncertain Saints

How About No

Whiskey Neat

Jack & Coke

Vodka On The Rocks

Bad Apple

Dirty Mother

Rusty Nail

The Kilgore Fire Series

Shock Advised

Flash Point

Oxygen Deprived

Controlled Burn

Put Out

I Like Big Dragons Series

I Like Big Dragons and I Cannot Lie

Dragons Need Love, Too

Oh, My Dragon

The Dixie Warden Rejects

Beard Mode

Fear the Beard

Son of a Beard

I'm Only Here for the Beard

The Beard Made Me Do It

Beard Up

For the Love of Beard

Law & Beard

There's No Crying in Baseball

Lani Lynn Vale

Pitch Please

Quit Your Pitchin'

Listen, Pitch (10-16-18)

The Hail Raisers
Hail No

Go to Hail

Burn in Hail

What the Hail

The Hail You Say

Hail Mary

The Simple Man Series

Kinda Don't Care

Maybe Don't Wanna

Get You Some

Ain't Doin' It

Too Bad So Sad

Bear Bottom Guardians MC

Mess Me Up

Talkin' Trash

How About No

My Bad (12-4-18)

One Chance, Fancy (1-15-19)

It Happens (2-12-19)

Keep it Classy (3-5-19)

PROLOGUE

No goats, no glory.
-T-shirt from Tractor Supply

Landry

5 years old

The needle hurt. The nice nurse said that it would, but she didn't have to tell me that it would. I already knew.

"When you wake up, you'll feel a little sore," the nice nurse lied.

I closed my eyes and tried not to cry.

My mommy and daddy didn't like it when I cried.

***

7 years old

"Hi there, Landry. Are you in any pain?" the nurse asked.

I nodded as I thought that I didn't know her name.

What was the point?

"Okay, I'll get you something." The nurse bustled out, and I took a quick glance around the room. My mommy and daddy weren't there.

They were likely two floors away with Lina.

They were always with Lina.

I shifted before I thought about it, and pain shot through my hips and a short gasp fell free of my lips.

I didn't cry, though. Crying never got me anywhere.

***

12 years old

"But, Mom! I don't want to do another one!" I cried out.

I didn't know why I was arguing. Hell, it never got me anywhere.

But God, I was just so tired.

I couldn't be a kid. I couldn't have fun. I couldn't go anywhere. Couldn't do anything.

I wanted cake! I wanted to go outside and play. I wanted to go to a bookstore and chance getting sick! I wanted a life!

"You don't get a choice in this, Landry Marine. You get to do what you're told because I'm the one who puts a roof over your head and food in your mouth," my father practically snarled.

I felt the anger burn in my throat, but what he said was true. He did pay for those things.

Though, I would gladly give up those two things if I was able to live the life I wanted to live.

My life—from the moment I was conceived in a test tube and implanted into the body of a woman who wasn't even my mother—had been for someone else's benefit.

It sure the heck wasn't mine.

I was created for the sole purpose of offering their daughter—the wonderful Lina—a chance at life.

Me? Well, the only reason they wanted me healthy was because if I wasn't healthy, I couldn't donate bone marrow to Lina when it was needed.

And it had been needed—many times.

But, lucky for everyone but me, Lina got better every time.

The only problem was that she would only get sick again six to twelve months later.

I was, of course, the last resort.

But, that didn't mean that I got to live my life in between those times when my sister wasn't considered sick.

Nope, not me.

I got to eat broccoli and asparagus. I only got fruits that weren't high in carbs.

White bread was a no-go, and I only ate the healthiest meals—lean chicken, whole grain rice.

I had my first and only bite of cake at a birthday party I was invited to, but my mother had slapped it out of my hand before I could get a second bite in.

That one had gotten me grounded for two months.

Not that it mattered.

I didn't have a life outside of my home anyway.

I was the most boring, in shape twelve-year-old on the planet.

My parents made sure of it.

***

15 years old

Everything hurt.

But there would be no pain medicine for me, though, on the off chance that I became addicted to it.

Those were my mother's words, not mine.

She watched over me like a hawk, and there was no way in hell that I'd ever get addicted to anything when she chose each and every thing that went into my mouth.

"Landry," my mother chided when I walked into the living room and immediately put my ass on the couch. "Go to your room. We don't want to listen to the television right now."

I looked around the room at my parents who'd walked in behind me.

Not that they'd be staying.

My mother would go to her solarium while my father went to his office.

There they'd spend the next couple hours working and or entertaining.

"Would you mind dropping this off in Lina's room on your way? She called and asked for a Happy Meal from McDonald's when you were in surgery."

I swallowed my anger and stood up, even though it hurt so bad that I could barely breathe.

Each time I donated, it only seemed to get worse and the recovery stretched out longer.

The pain lasted for weeks on top of weeks instead of the short intervals that I'd had in the beginning.

I was so young the first time that I underwent this procedure that I don't remember the recovery—I just remembered pain.

And that didn't even begin to factor in the depression that took me down for even longer.

"Sure," I croaked, grabbing the Happy Meal off the counter. "Are you sure I won't get germs on it?"

"Would you mind spraying the box down with Lysol, washing your hands, and then putting it out on a clean plate?" my father asked as he passed on his way to his office.

I wanted to throw it into the trash, but that wouldn't be very nice.

My sister didn't have a choice in how she was treated any more than I had a choice in how I was treated.

Which was why we lived in Mexico, in a house in the hills, with the very best of everything we could ever ask for because what they were doing to me was unethical. They would never allow me to be in a position where I could snitch on them that I wasn't willingly donating.

My parents could afford anything. Anything.

Paying off a doctor to perform the medical procedures? Check.

Buying a top of the line medical hospital room and round-the-clock nurses so that my sister could be treated at home when she had to be in isolation for three weeks prior to receiving my donation? Check.

Medical personnel willing to look the other way when I was too underweight to safely donate? Check.

Oh, and let's not forget the anti-depressants that I was on. We'll just act like we didn't hear that you were on them.

Yeah, my parents had everything in their front pocket, and their world revolved around their daughter.

Only, that daughter wasn't me.

***

17 years old

Being back in the United States felt weird.

Going to school felt even weirder.

I had exactly seven months left until I graduated. Until I turned eighteen.

Until I could run and never look back.

I knew I'd be found, but I would find a way.

Anything was possible.

"Do not eat that," my mother chided.

I ate the piece of candy and glared at her for good measure.

My mother narrowed her eyes, and I knew that it didn't matter how much I rebelled. She'd find a way to repay me.

And she did hours later by locking me in my bedroom and telling me to think about why I was being treated like a child.

***

18 years old

I walked across the stage with tears streaming down my cheeks.

I was free.

So freakin' free.

I had a bus ticket in my pocket.

I had eighty dollars cash that I'd stolen out of my father's wallet.

I had my diploma.

I was ready to run, and I was never looking back.

I only wished that my problems didn't have a way of catching up to me.

PROLOGUE II

Before you do anything stupid this weekend, just remember it's a three-day weekend and the judge won't be in until Tuesday. Just sayin'.
-Wade's secret thoughts

Wade

Five years ago

I saw her enter the classroom from across the room.

She was wearing tight blue jeans, a white t-shirt that fit her so tight I could make out every single curve, and a pair of white flip-flops that showed off her cute pink toenails.

I was teaching a criminal justice class for a friend, and I'd never been more excited than I was right then to tell my fellow cop and MC brother no, I wouldn't be taking over the class for him.

Why you ask?

Because I knew that girl was about to be mine.

The moment we were out of this classroom, I was going to ask her out on a date, and I couldn't do that if I was her teacher for the semester. The instant I saw those beautiful brown eyes of hers lift and take me in, I knew that I was lost.

So. Fucking. Lost.

And then there was the fact that she'd expressly violated the dress code for the class. Not that I wanted to object or anything, but she was supposed to be dressed in closed-toed footwear and have her hair up and away from her face.

The entire class was filled mostly with men, and honestly, I wasn't sure that she belonged in this class at all.

I wasn't sure why she was there, but I wasn't going to complain.

Then again, I could likely teach the class seeing as she would probably stay in here for one class and one class only once she found out what it was about.

My watch beeped, signaling that it was eight exactly, and I stood up and walked to the door, shutting and locking it.

I hated latecomers, and if anyone came to the door after I'd closed it, well, they'd be making a spectacle of themselves.

I made sure to pass directly in front of the desk that the girl—woman—had taken near the middle of the room, and nearly groaned when I smelled peaches.

I felt things inside of me start to tighten, and I was thankful that there was a podium at the front of the room to conceal my dick since I could already feel it getting hard.

Once I was in place, I pulled out the class roster and started to read off last names.

When I got to Hill, the woman's soft voice answered my harsh call.

"Here," came her lilting reply.

My eyes sliced to hers, and I saw her cheeks fill with color.

Well, imagine that.

Smirking, I finished off the rest of the roster and then tossed it onto the shelf beside me before taking a look around the room.

"I'm not your regular teacher," I started without preamble. "I'm taking over for my partner who's sick today. He has the flu, so be thankful that he's not the one here teaching you and infecting you with it."

A lot of masculine laughs filled the room, but they couldn't overpower the soft giggle that came from the girl.

Hill.

Our eyes met again, and it felt like a goddamn freight train had slammed straight into my chest when I saw the smile on her face.

I licked my lips and looked away, trying to find purchase where there wasn't any to be had.

"Anyway, this class is going to be fun this year," I paused. "At least it was when I took it a few years ago. There's no telling if Cass will be a fun teacher, or if he'll be the asshole he is the rest of the time I'm working with him."

The girl gasped, and I felt my lip quirk up at that.

Had she never heard anyone curse before?

"This class will teach you about hands-on tactics that you'll use during the police procedure such as when you're arresting a suspect, performing a traffic stop, or collecting evidence that you'll need to do during a traffic stop that turns into an arrest." I paused. "This is also something that you'll learn during the police academy, but more in-depth and widespread. Not to mention that whatever police department you work for will have their own policies and procedures in place."

I nearly laughed when I saw the woman's eyes glaze over as she took in all that I had to say.

No, this was definitely not the class for her…

An hour later, once I'd completed going over the syllabus on the topics that would be discussed this year, I sent the students on their way thirty minutes early.

Everybody got up and left, a few lingering to talk, except for one.

That student stayed at her desk, her head bowed as she stared at the course syllabus and tapped her fingers restlessly.

I found myself grinning as I walked up to her.

Stopping in front of her desk, I waited for her to notice that I was there.

When she finally did look up, I couldn't help myself.

"You didn't know what kind of class you were signing up for?" I asked conversationally.

She shook her head animatedly, that brown hair of hers falling into her eyes as she did.

I wanted nothing more than to reach up and push it away from her face.

"The counselor that signed me up for classes said that a lot of students took a criminal justice class when they needed to get full credit hours. So, I thought, why not? I'm not sure they take this one, though," she admitted. "I'm thinking that counselor was new or something, because it seems like this is a more advanced class, and you have to build on stuff you learned in previous classes to perform well in this one."

She was just the cutest thing.

I shrugged.

"Yes and no," I admitted. "Yes, it helps to have those other laws and rules to fall back on, but really this is more of a hands-on, what-to-do-in-certain-scenarios lab. It's not a to-take-this-class-you-must-take-the-prerequisites-first type of class, which is likely why the computer system allowed her to put you in here in the first place. It is, however, a more advanced class. Not really something you'll be able to use in your career if you're not planning on pursuing law enforcement as a profession."

She laughed. "Uh, no. I'm majoring in website design and computer programming, so, um, *not* law enforcement."

"No," I laughed out loud at her answer. "I don't think you'll need this course, but you're more than welcome to stay if you want."

She shrugged. "I might give it one more class, but honestly, it seems kind of advanced for, well, *me*, and I'm not sure that I want to take it. I'm more of a sit on my butt and watch the world around me type of person."

My lips twitched. "Nothing wrong with that, darlin'."

Her cheeks flushed again. "Well, I guess I better go. I have an hour until my next class, and I'm hungry."

I felt my heart leap. "You want to grab a bite to eat with me? I swear, I'm not a serial killer or anything."

Her laugh surprised both her and me. "No, I wouldn't think that a cop could do both, but for some reason I trust you. As long as you're not doing sushi for lunch, I'm down."

I'd never eat my favorite food again if it got her to go with me.

"No sushi," I promised.

Her smile was captivating. "Then that's a yes."

It was a yes for a whole lot of other things, too.

The day after our lunch, she said yes to a date. Two weeks after our first date, she said yes to being my girlfriend. Eight months after our first date, she said yes to becoming my fiancée. And six months after that, she said yes as she became my wife.

CHAPTER 1

*You're not a snack if everyone has had a bite.
You're a free sample.*

-Fun Fact

Landry

Two and a half years ago

"No, Wade," I snarled. "It's not just *that* easy."

He frowned. "What are you talking about? I realize that it's tough, and it's going to hurt, but baby, this is your sister! Your sister is your family. Your blood. You can't just leave her in need."

That was when I felt everything inside of me still.

"The first time I donated bone marrow to my sister, I was a toddler. Barely the age of two and a half," I said, almost in a whisper. "The second time, I was four. The third? Seven. Do you see a pattern, *Sergeant?*"

Wade frowned and tilted his head to the side, confusion spreading over his face.

"My parents had me to be their donor baby," I whispered. "They never wanted me. I was never allowed to be a child. I was a useful object to them."

Wade looked startled. "What do you mean by not being able to be a child?"

I laughed maniacally.

"I'm saying that I was bred to be their baby's saving grace," I hissed. "And I'm not doing it anymore. My sister is an asshole. My father's a conniving bastard, and my mother is the biggest bitch known to man. Don't you think that there's a reason that I've never spoken of them?"

He looked at me like I was crazy. "Honey, you told me that you had a falling out. But this is your sister."

I looked over at where my sister was sitting out on the front porch, silently crying her big, fat crocodile tears.

She'd always been good at them.

There was a time when I was younger that all she had to do was get that look on her face, and I'd be scared shitless.

Because if Lina wasn't happy, nobody was happy, least of all me.

There was always going to be hell to pay if a single tear fell down Lina's perfect cheek.

Lina also looked like a little China doll. She had perfect blonde curls, soft, milky white skin, blue eyes the color of a crayon, and she was tiny.

I, on the other hand, was none of those things but short.

I had brown hair to her blonde, brown eyes to her blue, freckled skin to her perfect complexion, and when I tried hard, I was also skinny.

Except, lately, I had been drinking beer and having the time of my life—living it like I'd always wanted to live it.

"I won't do it," I refused again, sounding petulant now.

I knew he didn't understand.

Deep down, Wade was a really good man.

He'd experienced a lot in his life. He was a cop and had seen some very bad things.

But, what he did not have, was a bad family.

His family was awesome. His mom was the best mother in the whole world, and his dad was the kind of father I'd only ever dreamed of having when I was younger.

God, even his brother was the best.

He had no clue what it was like to hate your family like I did.

Hell, the only reason he hadn't heard of them sooner was because my sister hadn't gotten sick enough to need me.

Had she, Wade would've learned the truth about who my family was a hell of a lot quicker.

"I'm going to tell her that you're thinking about it, and we can discuss it more later, okay?" Wade offered. "I don't want you to make any hasty decisions because you're overreacting."

Overreacting?

I wasn't overreacting.

Not even close.

"Whatever, Wade," I muttered, feeling defeated. "Go do what you have to do. I'm going to bed."

Wade went outside, and through the front windows, I saw Wade sit down and talk to Lina like she was a glass doll.

She wasn't.

She was hardcore. She was manipulative. She was…hugging my husband.

I stiffened when she threw herself into my husband's arms, and what did Wade do when that happened?

He wrapped those arms of his that were supposed to be wrapped around me and pulled her in tight.

That's when I knew I wasn't going to win the battle.

***

Three weeks later

"Why isn't your family here?" Wade asked, sounding concerned.

I snorted and turned my head on the pillow so it wasn't facing him anymore.

The last three weeks had been a lesson in control.

My parents and sister had put on good acts. They'd brought Wade into their arms and showed him just how nice they could be.

They'd put on the perfect show, and their efforts made Wade doubt me and everything I'd told him over the last few weeks to try to enlighten him to just how awful of a family I really had.

"Maybe I should call them," Wade offered.

I held my tongue.

The nurse poked me in the hand as she started an IV, and I closed my eyes and started to count to ten.

By the time I got down to five, I was fairly sure that I wasn't going to throw up.

"I'll be back. I'm going to call them," Wade murmured.

He disappeared out of the room, and I took a shaky breath.

"You might want to give me some valium," I offered up. "If you don't, I'm going to throw up, and you're going to have to put a new IV in because I'm going to freak out."

"Nervous?" she asked.

I swallowed so hard that I felt my throat burn. "Yes, sort of."

Not nervous, per se, at least not about the procedure anyway.

I was, as always, nervous about the pain.

The last time I'd felt the pain of this operation was seven years ago. Seven years to try to put the past behind me.

But I should've known better. The past never stayed in the past.

And I was born to endure the pain.

Pain that only got worse each and every time this procedure happened.

So, no, I wasn't nervous about the procedure itself. I just wasn't looking forward to the rest of it.

Or what I was going to do after—or where I was going to go.

All I knew was that I wasn't going home, or anywhere with Wade.

"Would you mind giving this to that man after the procedure has started?" I asked, handing her a thick envelope.

The nice nurse took it and grinned. "Sure thing, ma'am. I'm only a student nurse, though. I won't even be able to give you the meds you asked for without talking to the nurse supervising me today. But I'll let her know about your medication request and give the envelope to that man when you're taken back."

I looked at the student nurse's nametag. "Phoebe. That's a pretty name."

Phoebe smiled. "My sisters and I were named after the witches off of the old TV show, *Charmed*."

I grinned. "Did they use all the names?"

I loved *Charmed*.

"No, just three. Pru, Piper, and Phoebe. My mom wanted four, but life got in the way. In other words, no Paige for them."

I found myself smiling despite the turmoil of emotions churning in my gut over my impending procedure and what I knew would follow.

"Too bad."

Phoebe tapped my shoulder. "I'll see you soon."

I closed my eyes and pretended to sleep, hoping that by the time Wade got back, I would have had my dose of medication that would make me no longer care about what I was about to do.

***

Wade

"What is this?" I frowned at the thick envelope that the little nurse had just handed me.

"This is something your wife gave me to give to you once she was taken back." She paused. "I don't know any more than that, sir."

I opened the envelope, still pissed off that her family wasn't here. They didn't even answer the phone when I called and weren't here to see their daughter before her surgery. Hands shaking at how angry I was, I unfolded the papers.

The first thing I read stole the breath straight from my lungs.

FINAL DECREE FOR PETITION FOR DIVORCE FOR CAMP COUNTY JUDICIAL DEPARTMENT.

CHAPTER 2

Of all my mistakes, you were the mistakiest.

-Text from Landry to Wade

Wade

6 months ago

"Do you know why I pulled you over?" I asked carefully.

I mean, other than the fact that you moved in with my ex-wife the moment that I moved out.

The man offered up his license and registration but didn't respond, and I was actually kind of thankful for that.

Had I known it was him, I might very well have just let him go without pulling him over, because who wanted to talk to the man that was sleeping in his bed with his wife—ex-wife?

Not me, that was for sure.

I was an upstanding officer of the law. I was a biker. I was a good man.

Until it came to this guy.

And when I just so happened to observe the man that my ex-wife was sleeping with speeding like a motherfucker, I pulled him over because it was my duty to keep the citizens of this town safe.

"Here," Kourt Chamberlain said politely.

I took them and walked back to the SUV that I used and slid back inside of it.

The cool air conditioning hit my face like a soft caress, and I blew out a few quick breaths to try to regain my control.

After running the good doctor's information through the computer, I wrote him out a warning and walked it back to the car.

All the while I wondered if I was going to be able to control myself long enough to hand the warning ticket over.

I did.

Barely.

"Keep your speed down," I ordered.

Kourt nodded his head at me and offered me a slight head tilt before rolling up his window and driving away.

I stayed there long enough to wish that someone would T-bone his car and kill the bastard, then got back into my patrol car and drove back to the station.

The five-minute drive there, I tried to distract myself with thoughts of what I was going to do that day.

I had a witness that I needed to speak with, I had a few reports that I needed to type up, and I needed to call my insurance company and pay for the next six months of my truck insurance.

Landry fresh on my mind after stopping that bastard made me remember that she somehow was able to get better rates than I'd ever been able to get. When I'd asked her once shortly after we were married why she was always able to get discounts, she'd laughed and told me that being nice goes a long way.

And it was true.

Being nice did go a long way.

But, so did beating the shit out of people that pissed you off. I'd love nothing more than to string Kourt Chamberlain up by his testicles, and then put him near a fire ant bed while dousing him in sugar water.

My phone rang, and I groaned as I picked it up, thankful for anything that would distract me at this point.

"Hello?" I answered without checking to see who'd called.

"Um, yeah," the tweaker that I was supposed to be meeting in a half an hour tittered. "This Wade?"

He knew it was me just like I knew he was Raoul Karding.

"Yes," I answered, trying to conceal my impatience. "How can I help you, Raoul? We still on in half an hour?"

He made a grunting sound. "Yeah. Just wanted to make sure you'd be here."

I sighed. "Yes, Raoul. I'll be there. Just like I am every single time you ask."

Raoul grunted. "Okay, bye."

I rolled my eyes and hit End on the touch screen of the SUV's hands-free display, and then drove the rest of the way to the station wondering about why Raoul was so goddamn twitchy today.

I thought we'd gotten past the point of him thinking I was going to bail on him.

He'd been my contact in a child trafficking ring case for going on four weeks now, and it'd gotten to the point where I thought we'd established at least a modicum of trust.

"Hell," I muttered darkly, getting out of the SUV.

The moment my feet hit the ground, I heard someone call my name.

"Wade!"

I looked up and grinned when I saw Landry's sister, Lina, standing on the sidewalk next to the public library, two doors down from the police station that I was seconds away from walking inside.

"Hello, Lina," I said warmly.

Lina and Landry were polar opposites.

But Lina was sweet, and despite my being in a shit mood from having to deal with Landry's new man, I tried to conceal that when I went over and wrapped one arm around Lina in a side hug.

She felt nothing like Landry.

In fact, everything about this woman was totally different. I didn't even see a resemblance between the two of them.

That'd always surprised me.

From the moment that I'd first met her, I'd often wondered who Landry favored more. I wasn't sure that it was either of their parents. I could see Lina's resemblance with her mother, but Landry was everything that the other three weren't.

"How are you, Wade?" Lina asked, grinning wide.

I let her go and stepped back, putting my hands in my pockets.

Despite my not being married to Landry anymore, I still felt awkward if I happened to run into Lina or her parents around town when Landry wasn't around. The few times it had happened, I remembered the words that had spewed out of Landry's mouth the day that I confronted her on not donating her bone marrow to her sister.

And each time, I wondered if I hadn't pushed her in to making that decision, would we still be together.

"I'm doing okay," I admitted. "How are you? You're looking much better."

I was okay with the fact that Landry and I weren't together anymore if it meant that Lina got to live.

It sucked. It sucked so bad that sometimes I felt that I could hardly breathe.

But when another person's life was at stake, I would choose life over happiness any day.

Which was likely my downfall.

I was a protector and always would be. I was just sad that Landry never understood that.

"I'm feeling better." Lina shrugged. "I'm going to the doctor next week to make sure that I'm still cancer free, but I have high hopes that I'll be okay."

I did, too.

I didn't want to give up my marriage for nothing.

"Well, I better go. I have to go turn in my traffic stop book and get a new one," I grinned. "Take care of yourself."

Lina smiled and leaned slightly toward me.

I didn't move as she placed a chaste kiss on my cheek before saying, "Take care of yourself, Wade."

I didn't wait to watch her walk to the car.

Maybe if I would have, I would've seen the woman just a few cars down from Lina's, glaring murderously at me. A woman that wasn't supposed to care whether I was getting kisses, whether they were from that woman's sister or not.

But I didn't stay.

Instead, I walked to the station and turned my ticket book in.

Then I walked right back out because I had a few things that I was being forced to discuss with Raoul. Such as what he knew about the murder of the senator who died some time ago and who had been responsible for it—even though my hunch said that it was closely related to the case that I was currently investigating.

This particular case that I was working on involved a now-dead senator and a few local lawyers who were preying on teenagers and taking photos of their disgusting selves while doing it—literally.

Raoul was a low life who just so happened to need cash from time-to-time when those lawyers needed a little extra hand, and I was trying to get him to offer up his services where he could.

Which led to now, and me driving down in the seediest, shittiest, most cop unfriendly area in the damn city.

I should've changed out of my uniform, and I definitely should've switched to my bike.

But people would've known who I was just as easily on my bike, in my regular clothes, as they would have if I was in my uniform and driving my cruiser.

Sighing at the looks I was getting from the men and women that were gathered out on their porches, I kept driving until I got to the secluded spot that even I hadn't realized was there until Raoul told me about it and pulled over.

There I waited.

CHAPTER 3

I think I've seized the wrong fucking day.

-Landry's secret thoughts

Landry

I felt sick to my stomach, as I always did when I saw Wade.

Though today's stomachache was tenfold seeing as when I saw Wade, I had also seen my sister—who had known I was there when she'd gone out of her way to call out to Wade.

I hated her.

God, how I hated her.

I'd like nothing more than to wish her disappearance from this planet.

Was it not good enough that she'd taken my childhood? Did she also have to take what little happiness I had found in adulthood, too?

Hell, she already had stolen my husband—even if she hadn't done it in the normal way by sleeping with him.

Honestly, I thought that might've been easier, had that happened.

At least then I wouldn't have to feel like an awful person for leaving him.

Though my reasons were justified—at least to me—they weren't to him.

Over the three weeks before my procedure, I'd spoken until I was blue in the face about not wanting to do it, about how I'd done it so many times before. All the while, he held strong.

He urged me to do it anyway. Just one more time.

Except, I knew it wouldn't be one more time. It was never one more time.

I remembered Wade's face as he looked at me for the first time after our divorce as if I'd betrayed him.

But he didn't understand—and honestly, I don't think he wanted to understand.

He always saw the good in people, and probably always would.

I slammed the door to my house—the one Wade ordered me to keep—and wished I'd never agreed to it.

He hadn't wanted anything. Not a single thing.

Not the house we'd bought together, not the new car. Not the business we'd started or the money we'd managed to save over the time we were married.

Not a single thing but his clothes and his bike—which I couldn't drive anyway, otherwise I was sure that he'd try to get me to take that, too.

Hell, he'd almost made me keep the dog, too.

And that one I had put my foot down on.

I would not take his dog.

I refused.

As much as I loved Butters, I would not take him away from the man who had been his human for five years before I'd come along.

Nope. No. Nuh-uh.

And when Butters had died just a short six weeks after we'd finalized our divorce, things had been pretty bad for a short time.

I'd gone to check on Wade multiple times, only to stop myself well before making it to his street.

He didn't need me making things worse.

Hell, neither did I.

Each time I saw him, it only made me feel worse for leaving.

But, when I'd left home at the age of eighteen, I'd made a promise with myself.

I knew that if I didn't start putting me first, I wouldn't be on this Earth much longer.

I knew that I was going to fall apart just like I had at the age of seventeen.

I'd break hard, too, just like I had then.

Shortly after my seventeenth birthday, when I didn't get a car like my sister had gotten on her seventeenth birthday, I realized that I never was meant to be anything but a means to an end for my family.

Hell, I would've been happy with a damn cupcake with a candle in it at that point.

And, I'd been so depressed that I had actually thought about committing suicide.

I hadn't succeeded, obviously.

But that was only because of Kourt.

He'd found out about my attempt because I'd told him I was going to do it. He had stolen a wad of cash from his parents, as well as one of his parents' cars, and had hauled ass my way.

Luckily, at the time, Kourt had been in his second year of medical school and had been able to get to me in time to talk me out of doing anything so permanent. From there, he'd stayed with me to make sure that I was okay, and a bond had formed.

One that, if I hadn't had it, I only would have thought about doing it again.

My phone chimed with a text message, and I pulled it out of my purse, finding my first smile for the day.

Kourt: So, I almost got a ticket today.

I grinned and called him, knowing he only texted because he thought I was still at work. I wasn't and hadn't been for over half an hour.

"Oh, yeah? Almost? What were you doing?" I asked the moment he answered his phone.

"I was speeding." He sounded tired. "And you'll never guess what happened."

I found myself grinning, though only partially. "You got a ticket?"

"No," he answered. "I got a warning. From your ex-husband."

My insides felt like they'd exploded as everything tightened at the mention of my ex.

"He only gave you a warning?" I asked in surprise.

"Yeah," Kourt explained. "Can you believe it?"

"No," I admitted. "Are you sure he didn't give you a ticket and you just don't realize it?"

He snorted. "I can clearly see what it says. WARNING is written at the top in big bold letters." He paused. "My guess is that he gave me a warning because he didn't want me to contest it and have to see me again in court."

I snorted. "That sounds like Wade. He's always put a lot of thought in everything he does."

I missed him.

God, how I missed him.

"He looked like he'd rather kill me than hand me that warning." Kourt laughed then. "I felt like throwing up. I seriously almost did when I saw it was him. I swear to God, Landry. He could totally kick my ass. Then he'd break my surgeon hands, and I wouldn't be able to save lives!"

I rolled my eyes.

Kourt was, indeed, a surgeon. He was also a really good one who could've gone anywhere, but he came here to do his residency and I followed him. He had moved in with me when my house was more convenient than the apartment he was renting.

Why were we such good friends?

Because we were one and the same.

Kourt and I had both grown up in almost identical situations to each other. The only differences between our upbringing had been that he grew up in India while I grew up in Mexico. Kourt had gotten free a hell of a lot faster than I had, also.

Although that was due to his brother being born, who also happened to be a match for their eldest brother, who had leukemia. His parents were able to split the time in between both brothers.

Though, where Kourt and I had survived—barely—Kourt's brother, Beaux, had not.

Kourt and Beaux had both been put through the same thing that I had been put through—multiple rounds of bone marrow donations attempting to save a sibling. However, where Kourt and I had been able to mentally handle the strain of the endless rounds of attempts to cure, Beaux had taken his own life rather than live the way he was forced to. I had Kourt to thank for being able to handle the stress.

Sadly, Kourt still felt a lot of guilt over it and would continue to for the rest of his life.

Where Lina had been a right bitch who had ultimately survived, Kourt's brother, Monty, that he'd been donating to, had died a few weeks after his last bone marrow transplant. His body had rejected it, and that had been what ultimately killed him.

"I gotta go," he said quickly. "Love ya."

"Love you, too," I said to dead air.

I rolled my eyes at that.

I should be used to the fact that Kourt hung up on me every freakin' time he was on the phone with me, but I wasn't.

Honestly, it ticked me off.

It didn't matter what he was doing, or whether it was an emergency or not.

He'd hang up without so much as a goodbye, and sometimes before I even realized that goodbye was on the horizon.

But, since it was usual for him, I didn't worry about it.

Instead, I got to work—to my second job.

My first job was my boring job. The one that made me money and provided me with endless blood pressure problems.

I owned a daycare—another thing that Wade and I had started, but he'd let me keep in the divorce—and worked there four out of five days a week—mostly because my workers called in sick at least once a week, forcing me to work even if I didn't want to.

Owning your own business was exhausting. You may wish that you are just the boss, but there are so many things that you have to take care of personally that sometimes you don't get to do just the fun things like you wanted to.

Though it was a very satisfying job, it also made me lonely.

I got to see everyone else's kids, got to love on them and squeeze them, but never got to take them home.

I knew without a shadow of a doubt that I'd forever be alone.

Just as I was about to begin answering emails and starting to gather donations for my second job—the actual love of my life—my dog rescue, my phone rang.

I frowned at it and considered not answering it, but since it was the hospital and likely Kourt, I did.

Only, it wasn't Kourt.

It was the emergency room.

"Mrs. Johnson, I'm calling about your husband coming in with a gunshot wound…"

***

Shot in the thigh. Lacerations to his liver and broken ribs from being beaten. A concussion that was considered quite severe. A fractured foot.

The list went on and on, and by the time the doctor was finished explaining the full list of his injuries, I nearly broke down and cried.

"He's in surgery right now to remove the bullet from his leg. Once we're finished, we'll call down here and let you know how surgery went."

That was two hours ago.

I'd been sitting in the surgical waiting room for what felt like forever, surrounded by men that I knew despised me.

The moment that Wade and I had broken up, I'd become numero uno on their dislike list.

At one time, I'd been the wife. At one time, I'd been loved.

At one time…

Needless to say, if I saw one of them, they went out of their way to avoid being in my presence.

It hurt.

It hurt even more due to the fact that they'd called me first, and when I'd shown up, all of them had looked at me not only as if I did *not* belong there, but that I was also unwelcome.

Honestly, if they could wish me gone from a room, I'd have disappeared hours ago.

To make matters worse, everyone was talking about me like I wasn't even in the room.

I could hear the woman that was with Rome speaking about me—complete untruths—as she tried to get more information on me. Rome was talking too softly to her for me to hear his replies, but I was sure those were just as untruthful as the things coming out of the woman's mouth.

Each word that came out of their mouths caused me to hunch further and further into myself.

There I sat, in the corner, praying that Wade didn't die.

Praying that one day, being a cop in this world wouldn't automatically make you hated.

I'd just finished asking God to take me instead—*because what was I good for, anyway?*—when a commotion had me lifting my head.

That's when I saw a gun aimed at me and thought, this must be it.

It hadn't been the way that I expected to go.

Honestly, I always expected that I'd die on an operating table.

The man fired the gun.

I raised my hand as if that would protect me, and I felt fire race through me moments later.

The entire room went electric.

Another shot was fired.

And then another.

And another.

And another.

All the while, I felt like laughing.

Up until this point, I'd always thought that God wasn't listening to me. Thought that he didn't care.

I guess I was wrong.

CHAPTER 4

I'm not on drugs. I'm just weird.

-Coffee Cup

Wade

I opened my eyes to darkness—at least semi-darkness anyway.

Everything hurt.

My face. My teeth. My toes and elbows.

Honestly, there wasn't a single thing on my body that didn't ache.

I rolled my head and yep, even my neck hurt.

Super.

When I turned my neck to the other side, my eyes caught on something—a lumpy form—and I blinked, trying to get my eyes to focus.

My hand twitched, and that was when I felt the remote in my hand.

Closing my fingers around it, I lifted it up and sat up slightly, finding that it was the intercom thingy that allowed you to connect to the nurses' station, as well as turn on the lights and adjust the bed.

I hit the lights, and the harsh bright glow of the ones right above my face had me blinking rapidly to dislodge the stars now flashing in my eyes.

I blinked once more and then tried to focus on the lumpy form that was actually a woman—my woman—or my former woman.

Landry was passed out in a chair, her upper body and head plastered against the soft weave of the blanket that was covering three-quarters of my body.

And, unlike when we used to be married, the stark overhead light didn't affect her in the least.

Guess her hating me wasn't the only thing that had changed since she'd last been in my bed.

I found myself getting irrationally angry over the light.

When I had been married and sharing a room with Landry, I would have to set my shit out the night before and get dressed out in the living room after being very sure to not only close the door—but do it as quietly as possible.

Landry was a very light sleeper.

So light, in fact, that any number of things could wake her up in the morning.

The water running in our bathroom. A cabinet closing. The zipper of my pants. Hell, even making coffee had woken her up.

I'd tiptoed around that place when I'd gotten ready for work, all because I hated waking her.

And here she was, bright light shining in her face, and she was sleeping like a baby.

It shouldn't have made me so angry, but it did.

I shifted my foot next to her face, bumping her lightly.

She came up with a cry of pain, tears already streaming down her face, and her bandaged hand clutched to her chest.

And that was when I realized that she'd been hurt, and I'd just kicked her.

"Fuck, Landry. I'm sorry," I apologized, reaching out to her.

She blinked a few tears from her eyes and then focused on me for a few long seconds.

Her mouth fell open, and she stared at me in awe. "You're awake!"

And then she was throwing herself forward.

Before I could so much as get my mouth open to demand her to tell me what was wrong, she was on me.

The minute she hit my chest, her face burying itself in the crook of my neck, her tears started coming faster. So fast that I could feel them running down my neck and curling around my shoulder blade to disappear into the sheet beneath my battered and bruised body.

A battered and bruised body that felt like it'd been run over by a log truck and every single log it had been hauling had broken free and rolled over me as well.

"I'm so glad that you're all right," Landry whispered. "They called me to tell me you were shot. Apparently, I'm still listed as your medical emergency contact. I raced up here, and they'd already taken you to surgery. You scared the crap out of me."

I had hundreds of questions looming through my brain that I wanted answers to.

The first question was, why was she here, not only beside me but half on my bed? Secondly, did she still love me like I loved her? Three, was that what it took? Me getting hurt for her to talk to me other than a few civil words here and there as I helped her with the daycare?

She hadn't held an actual conversation with me in the time that we'd been separated.

My thoughts then progressed into what should have been my first question, what had happened to me? And the last thoughts, why the hell did it feel so good to have her in my arms? Did she feel the same way when I touched her?

My mind had been thrown into turmoil with the thought that Landry was here beside me. So, finally, I settled with asking the question that was bothering me the most.

"What happened to your hand?" I rasped.

My voice didn't sound like it usually did, and I had it answered moments later as to why.

"Don't talk too much," she ordered. "They just took the tube out of your throat that was helping you breathe. Are you feeling okay?"

She hadn't answered my question, which made me nervous.

I wouldn't be answering any of her questions until she answered mine first.

"What happened to your hand?" I repeated.

When she went to pull away, I latched onto the long hair that was laying on my shoulder, holding her in place.

I saw her eyes dilate, and I knew what she was thinking.

I fucking loved her long hair. It was one of my favorite things about her.

When she was around—when we were married of course—her hair was always touching me in some way.

If I was close enough to her, my hand was wrapped around her braid, or my fingers were sifting through her ponytail. God, I loved it. There was something about having her hair in my hand that made me feel comforted, and I couldn't tell you why.

And it always would.

Just like I'd always love her.

"I don't know," she hesitated. "The doctors said not to get you riled up. I have a feeling if I told you, you may get upset."

I growled, letting her hear my frustration.

Ignoring the pain that the act caused, I sat up and pulled her hair, forcing her to come closer while also pulling her over until she was now sitting on the bed next to my leg.

I would address the searing pain in my thigh later. I'd also try to figure out why my dick felt so goddamn funny, too.

But for now, I wanted to know what in the goddamn hell had caused Landry harm. God help the motherfucker that had caused it.

"Tell. Me."

Landry narrowed her eyes and lifted her lip in a silent snarl. "Don't tell me what to do, bossy pants. I wasn't the one that nearly almost died. You were."

I opened my mouth to tell her exactly what I thought about that statement, but I was interrupted when Bayou came into the room, clearing his throat.

"She was shot in the hand," he said without preamble. "Through and through between her thumb and pointer finger—right through the webbing and missed every single bone. The man that you were investigating—one of the lawyers involved in the pedophile ring, got pissed that the other lawyer sang like a canary and got a plea bargain in exchange for narcing on his fellow criminals. He came and shot up the entire waiting room. Nobody died, but your girl there took a bullet straight through her hand."

I looked at Landry's hand and felt something inside of me sour.

"Bayou got shot in the side, took a chunk of meat out that required stitches," Landry muttered darkly. "But you don't see him admitting that, do you?"

My eyes flicked to Bayou, then back to Landry. "I wasn't asking him what was wrong. I was asking you."

Because honestly, I could give a fuck what happened to Bayou. Bayou was a grown fucking man. Landry, on the other hand, was my wife—ex-wife. She meant the entire world to me—even if she'd left me.

I couldn't say the same for Bayou.

Although I was concerned that he'd been hurt.

But still. There was a large difference between Bayou and Landry, and there always would be.

She shrugged. "Whatever."

My lips twitched, and I let her go. Reluctantly.

She looked just as hesitant to move away from me as I had been at letting her go.

I almost reached for her again, but Bayou cleared his throat and asked, "There anything you two need?"

Landry looked down at her hands and shook her head. "I should probably go."

And before I could open my mouth to protest, she was out of the room and out of my life all over again. At least, she would try to be.

I hadn't talked to her that much since the divorce—though that was her doing and not mine. I at least tried. And then she'd been shielding her feelings so hard that I had been left reeling.

She'd acted as if she wasn't affected at all. As if I was just an annoying piece of gum she'd just scraped off her shoe.

But looking at the tears in her eyes as she hauled ass out of the room, I knew better than most that women didn't cry if they were unaffected.

They also didn't come and wait at the hospital for news of their ex-husband, either.

"That girl," Bayou said, causing me to turn my attention to him. "Never seen her so fucking scared."

I didn't know what to say to that.

"And she yelled at the man she lives with. He was trying to take care of her hand, and all she wanted to do was get to you." He laughed. "Was obvious as hell that she still had feelings for you, and she didn't care who knew it. Not even the man that she's living with."

I snorted. "Yeah, well. If she felt that way, then why is she living with him and not me?"

A loud snort had me turning to the door once again.

Startled, I looked up to find the last person in the world I ever thought I'd see in my hospital room.

"Have you ever asked yourself why she *was* living with me?" the man who had stolen my wife away from me asked, standing in the doorway.

I scowled. "What are you doing here?"

"You're on my floor, goober," Kourt replied. "And you didn't answer my question. Have you ever asked yourself why she was living with me?"

I didn't want to answer that question. In fact, I'd rather light myself on fire and put myself out with gasoline.

I frowned. "You mean other than the obvious?"

Kourt scoffed. "That's a big negative, Wade. I'm not with your wife. I've never been with Landry. In fact, I've never wanted to be with your wife—at least not in *that* way. We just share a bond, and we keep each other on track. Maybe you should lay there and listen to what I have to say."

"Why would you do that?" I asked.

"Because today, I realized that you're both stupid," he answered as he settled into the chair at my bedside. "I realized that after you both were severely injured and it could have been life threatening the way the bullets were flying in that waiting room. Both of you were so concerned about each other. Y'all are likely to be the kind of people who follow each other into death. And if y'all are going to do something like that, then you both should probably be together in the first place."

The last thing I wanted to do was talk to this man about my life, but it didn't look like I had much choice in the matter seeing as Kourt was now sitting down and I was fairly sure that if I attempted to stand up to get away from him, I'd fall flat on my face.

"Fine," I moved until I was up farther in the bed and ignored the pain that shafted straight through my thigh the moment that I did. "Enlighten me. I'm just not promising that I'll like what you have to say."

He laughed harshly, without humor. "Oh, I don't doubt it for a second. The moment that I 'enlighten' you, you're going to lose your shit."

I had a feeling that I wasn't going to like what he had to say either, but as it turned out, it was not for the reasons that I'd thought it would be.

I looked over at Bayou to gauge his reaction to the comment and found him leaning against the wall, appearing as if he was uninterested even though I knew damn well and good that he was.

Bayou had adored Landry, and sadly, he'd had to choose sides when we'd divorced. He had chosen me.

"We met each other online years ago, on Reddit, actually. Then, she moved here because I was here doing my residency." He paused. "But at first, it was both of us just talking, expressing our frustrations online that started all of this."

I already didn't like where this was going.

"We were both on the verge of killing ourselves when we met up." He frowned. "She was very depressed and talking to me about having a plan. I knew that if she had a plan to kill herself, it was likely that she would accomplish it. That was when I met her face-to-face for the first time."

Every single thing that'd been going through my mind—the pain in my thigh, the throbbing in my skull, the pain in my heart at watching the woman that I loved leave me—it was all gone. It was replaced with a sudden horrible sense of dread that made my already uneasy breaths stall in my chest.

"I've wanted to have this discussion with you for a very long time," Kourt said calmly. "But she made me promise to keep my distance. I was not, under any circumstances, to ever tell you a thing without her express permission."

I felt something inside of me clench.

I wasn't sure that I wanted to know what he was about to tell me.

I had a feeling that I was not going to like it.

"How much do you know about her family?" he asked.

"You mean other than her sister having leukemia, and them living in Mexico for her first seventeen years of life?" I clarified.

My voice sounded raspy as hell, and I would kill for a drink of water.

Kourt got up and handed me one before I could even think to ask.

I didn't want to drink it on general principle alone, but then I'd just look petty, and I wasn't normally a petty person.

Then again, the man living with my wife, living the life that I wanted to be living, and he was now handing me water while looking at me like I was a small child that needed to be taken care of.

"I'm sure that you think the Hills are good people," Kourt started. "But they're not. They're awful people."

I frowned. "I haven't had many dealings with them. I know I was upset when they didn't visit Landry in the hospital when she was donating bone marrow to her sister. Sure, I see them around town. Actually, saw Lina recently. Was it this morning?"

"Oh, yeah, you saw her this morning. I know all about that visit with Lina," Kourt rumbled.

I would've snorted had I had the energy.

At this point, I had just enough to keep my eyes open and that was it.

"How about I tell you how we met, and we'll go from there," he explained, sensing my tiredness. "It all began when we found each other online. We were in an online community for bone marrow donors. Landry and I were the only members of that forum who had endured what we had experienced, and that was probably why we'd latched onto each other so fast.

"Everybody else was so proud of themselves, telling everyone that they felt so good about donating, while Landry and I...*weren't*." He laughed bitterly, his eyes going far away like he was no longer seeing what was right in front of him. "We bonded over an infection that we both got after one of our donations, and from there we became great friends. She became my sounding board, and I became the only person who understood how much—and why—she hated her family, because I felt exactly the same way."

I closed my eyes and felt another stab of guilt go through me.

I hadn't intended for that to happen. I hadn't intended to make her think that Lina should come first.

I'd only been thinking about how Lina might die if she didn't get the bone marrow transplant that she needed. Sure, she'd voiced the fact that she didn't want to do the transplant, but I honestly couldn't get over the letting her sister die part just because she had a couple of bad experiences donating.

God, I was such a fucking dumbass sometimes.

"I'm not telling you this to make you feel bad. I'm telling you this because you need to understand exactly where she's coming from so you'll know how to fix it," he explained.

I nodded once. "Keep going."

"While we were becoming friends, we bonded over how shitty our parents were. I'll save my story for another time, and just go ahead and tell you exactly what she told me," he explained. "They had Landry for the sole reason of helping to keep her sister, Lina alive." He paused. "Lina had been fighting leukemia since she was an infant. Landry was two years old when she first donated bone marrow to Lina. This was when they moved to Mexico, because no doctor in the United States would conduct a harvest from a donor as young as Landry. They found a doctor in Mexico who was willing, and from there Landry became their unwilling donor any time that Lina needed it, which was too much for her. I'm not saying that Lina hasn't suffered, because she has, but it was different for Landry. She suffered tremendously, and she was robbed of her childhood, all without her consent."

Bayou shifted, drawing my attention briefly before I returned it to Kourt.

"What else?"

Kourt shrugged. "The usual. She was treated like a commodity, brought to this Earth solely for the purpose of providing stem cells for her sister. In between donations, Landry was allowed to get an education. However, she was not allowed to play sports—because sports could be dangerous and could possibly hurt Landry—and

Lina by association." I looked down at my hands as Kourt continued. "She wasn't allowed to eat anything other than what was provided for her. It was strictly monitored so she was the healthiest she could be. All of this was planned so she would be ready if Lina needed a transfusion. But, everyone deserves a treat or a special meal now and then, and Landry never got that. If by chance, Landry put anything her parents deemed 'unhealthy' in her mouth, her mother punished her for it, *severely*."

I remembered the cake at our wedding. How Landry had sat for hours and tasted each and every flavor.

How annoyed I'd been at the end because she couldn't choose.

And now I felt like an even bigger pile of shit.

God, I'd really fucked up.

Who didn't allow their child to eat junk once in a while?

"Forget about going to normal places that kids went, like the movies or roller skating, or doing normal things with friends, like sleepovers or birthday parties, because she didn't have any. She was homeschooled and the only person that she ever talked to was her tutor. Her parents didn't spare her a second of their time, and neither did her sister when she was healthy. There was no warmth, no affection, no love in her life from them at all, ever. Honestly, I think Lina hated Landry because Landry was healthy, and she wasn't. Which is kind of ironic, really, because Landry hated Lina for the same reason." He paused. "This is where it starts getting tough, you ready?"

I laughed humorlessly. "That other stuff wasn't tough enough?"

He looked at me like I was naïve.

"A couple of years before I came into the picture, Landry started to show signs of depression. She stopped eating altogether, and she became very unhealthy. She was anorexic because that was literally the only thing she could control—what she put into her body. There were times over the years that her mother and father had her force-fed with an NG tube—a little tube that goes down your nose, down your throat, and straight into your stomach. Then she couldn't even control that anymore." He frowned. "It was at that point that she considered suicide. Considered it until she turned seventeen when she actually thought seriously about attempting it."

I felt my eyes sting.

Who could blame her?

"That's where I came in. I'd been in medical school for a little over three years at that point. Took me two hours to get there. Broke into her place through a side window. Fortunately, she was holding the bottle of pills in her hands and hadn't taken any yet. I don't think either of us truly realized that she was so much younger than me until I arrived and saved her. Her parents didn't even try to help her with counseling so, I continued to monitor her and talked to her every day. They were pissed as hell, though. The last year that she lived with them was torture for her. When she turned eighteen, she followed me here where I was doing my residency, and we've been with each other ever since…until you. When you came in the picture, I was completely and utterly forgotten. It was the most beautiful thing that I've ever witnessed."

And I'd hurt her.

"You were her saving grace. Her miracle. The man who was always supposed to put her first…and then you chose Lina over her, and she just…broke."

When he put it like that, after everything he'd just told me, I couldn't blame her one bit for leaving.

Didn't blame her at all.

At least not anymore.

"I can see you're hurting." Kourt stood and went for the pain pump that was at my side. "Press the button in your left hand."

I hadn't even realized that I had a button in my left hand, but after glancing down and seeing that I did, indeed, have the button in my hand, I pressed it.

"I'm sure that you're going to have questions," he said softly. "Don't hesitate to ask. We work opposite shifts, and I'm normally here when she's at home. I'm at home when she's at work. I'll leave my cell phone number here in your phone." He informed me as he picked my phone up and typed his information in without asking.

With that, he left and didn't once look back.

If he had, he'd have seen the devastation that his words left me with written plain as day on my face.

I felt utterly broken.

"I think we both failed her, man," Bayou said softly.

Yeah, I think we—*I*—did, too.

CHAPTER 5

Fool me once, fuck you forever.

-Text from Landry to Wade

Landry

My hand hurt.

My hand hurt really bad.

In fact, on a pain scale of one to ten, I'd rank it at about a seventy.

"You okay?"

I gasped and looked up, finding the last person I ever thought that I'd see standing in front of me.

"Yeah," I nodded at Bayou. "I'm okay. My hand hurts, is all."

It'd been two weeks since I'd been shot—since Wade had also been shot—and it felt even worse today than it had when it'd first happened.

Hell, even Bayou had been shot. It'd been a flesh wound, but still.

We were just three peas in a pod.

"Gonna hurt for a while, I expect," Bayou grunted and took a seat on the bench next to me.

I was on lunch break from the daycare, and I'd rather be anywhere but where I was at.

I used to love the place, and what it represented, but now? Well, now I wasn't so excited about coming here every day. It was a pain in the ass, and I was beginning to resent it.

Not to mention all the hassle that came with it.

Parents being late on making payments. Kids coming in sick and passing it along to me. Employees coming in late for work, or hell, not coming in at all. Things going wrong—such as the oven breaking last week, or the toilets overflowing.

As much as I enjoyed seeing the children every day, their smiling faces and laughter…it wasn't enough anymore.

"How do you know it's going to hurt for a while?" I asked. "Done it often?"

He snorted. "This bullet wound was my third—and hopefully last. The first two I sustained a couple of months into my first tour. Took one to the lower calf, and one to the upper arm. They all fucking hurt, but I suspect that none of them hurt as much as taking one through your hand."

"How do you know?" I challenged.

"I know based on usage levels. Your hand is probably one of the most used out of all your body parts." He moved until he was perched on the bench beside me, his long legs stretched out in front. "You do a lot more with your hand than you realize. Drive. Eat. Sleep on it. Style your hair. The hand has more nerves than other body parts, also."

I gave him a droll look. "My hair looks bad, doesn't it?"

He snorted. "It's cute. Just like you."

I laughed at that. "You're terrible."

I felt like crying.

Bayou hadn't spoken to me so much in a long time.

I missed him.

I hadn't realized how much until that very moment.

Hell, that only made me miss Wade all the more.

"Why are you sitting out here all alone?" he asked.

"Why are you sitting out here all alone?" I countered.

I'd seen him, of course.

He'd been sitting on the park bench across the entire park. The bench that I usually sat at because it was the furthest away from the daycare.

If I sat too close, the workers sometimes came out to ask me questions despite it being my lunch break, and I wasn't in the mood to deal with whether they thought I should be open for Labor Day or not.

"I was here first," he countered.

That he was.

"True."

"Dropped Wade off at physical therapy today. I was waiting for him to call and let me know that he's ready to be picked up…" he began.

I snorted. "Wade probably took a freakin' taxi. If you've been waiting, that means he's been gone for a while."

Bayou frowned, then pulled out his phone to dial a number. I assumed it was the hospital.

When he spoke to whoever was on the other end of the line, his frown got ferocious.

"Fuck, okay. Thank you."

Then he hung up, glaring at me lightly.

"Why didn't you go get him if you knew that he was going to do that?" he accused.

I snorted. "I don't know what made you think that Wade and I talk, but we don't," I told him bluntly. "In the hospital, that was the first time I was close enough to speak to him in a very long time."

That was by design, of course.

It was hard as hell to be around the love of my life and not want him.

He'd broken my heart, of course, but that didn't mean that I hated him.

I didn't.

I loved him.

I just needed him to love me more than what he was able to give me.

It was selfish, yes.

But for my sanity, as well as peace of mind, that was the path that I chose in life.

And if that made me unhappy, then so be it.

I was not living my life for anyone else anymore.

At least, that'd been what I thought up until I'd heard that Wade was shot.

Then all my good intentions flew out the window.

He'd scared the absolute crap out of me, and the thought of a world without Wade in it made me sad.

Too sad.

Way sadder than a person should be when they were divorced from said person.

"Seems like that's a little excessive, don't you think?"

Was it?

How About No

I didn't think so.

At least, at the time I hadn't.

Now, I wasn't sure what I felt.

With the distance we had between us, it became a lot easier to avoid him than it had back then.

It'd been two years since our divorce had been finalized, and each month—hell, each day—had been an exercise in control.

I missed my best friend.

I missed him, and I knew that it was my fault that I missed him.

But fuck…when he'd been hurt.

I'd seen my life flash before my eyes, and it'd been a lonely, desolate feeling seeing my older self so bitter and all alone.

"You're thinking some hard stuff over there, girl," Bayou rumbled. "There a reason for that frown the size of Texas?"

I snorted. "Just thinking that I'm kind of stupid."

"We're all stupid," he told me, sounding so sure that I paused to fully listen. "Some of us just get over being dumb faster than others."

I agreed with that wholeheartedly.

But shit.

There was getting over being stupid, and then there was getting over being me. I couldn't change who I was. Not when it was so thoroughly ingrained in my psyche.

"I…"

My phone rang, interrupting me.

And my heart skipped a beat because I hadn't heard that ringtone in so long that it physically hurt to hear it.

I hadn't heard it since Wade and I had still been a couple.

How do I live without you…

I snatched it up before the song that I associated with Wade continued to play, and answered it as fast as I possibly could.

"Hello?"

The last person in the world I expected to be on the other end of the line was my ex-husband. God, it'd been so long since he'd called.

"Landry," Wade's deep, melodic voice practically purred into my ear.

God, every single freakin' time I heard his voice I wanted to melt into a puddle of goo at his feet.

I didn't know what it was about the deep resonance of this man's voice that set my blood on fire but, swear to God, all he had to do was say my name sometimes and I wanted him.

"Hey," I said softly, looking up to find Bayou staring across the street at someone. "What's up?"

"I had a call from my Pop today," he said without preamble. "Do you think you can spare the day tomorrow to go with me somewhere?"

Like I'd ever tell him no.

Hell, he didn't even have to explain.

"Sure," I said without any further thought. "What time?"

"Eight. No, seven. I'll pick you up at your place," he stated.

I looked down at my suddenly trembling hands. "Okay," I agreed. "See you then."

I heard the click of dead air seconds later, and I was left staring at my phone like it was an object from outer space instead of the lifeline that kept me entertained throughout the day.

"I'm not sure how I ever survived before I got my first phone," I murmured, trying to dislodge the lump in my throat that hearing my ex-husband's voice caused.

"I remember a time where I had to read the tampon boxes when I took a shit," he said. "We didn't have these fancy phones with the world at our fingertips, keeping us entertained like we do nowadays. I knew all about toxic shock syndrome, thanks to my sister leaving her feminine hygiene products out. I also remember reading the goddamn toilet cleaner label."

I started to snicker. "No reading shampoo bottles for you, eh?"

He winked at me and stood, his eyes once again going across the street.

I saw a woman there, kitted out in high heels and a flowy dress, drawing on the storefront windows with shoe polish. "Who's that?"

Bayou shrugged. "New bakery chick. She opens at the end of the month."

"How do you know?" I squinted my eyes to see if I could see anything on the window's storefront that would tell me what it was.

Other than the half-drawn cupcake, I couldn't see any distinguishing markers that would give that information out freely.

"She comes to visit a man once a week at the prison," he answered, his eyes still captivated. "I have to throw away her goddamn cupcakes, too."

I gasped. "Why?"

He looked down at me then.

"Have you ever thought about smuggling razor blades in cupcakes? What about lube?" he asked, tilting his head to the side.

I opened my mouth and then closed it. "Did she? No, I mean the answer is no," I admitted. "Did she hide something in the cupcake?"

He shook his head. "No. But it's been done before. Fool me once…" With that, he left, offering me a wink. "Take care of yourself, girl."

I lifted my hand to wave but stopped halfway when I felt the entire thing cramp up.

My stomach bottomed out as my hand went into a violent spasm, and I barely stopped the cry of pain from falling past my lips.

Luckily, I managed, because Bayou didn't turn around or catch the pain.

Then again, I wasn't sure if it was because I'd held the cries in, or because there was a hawk in the air drawing his attention away from me.

Sighing in pain, I shoved what was left of my no longer appetizing lunch into my sack and stood up.

All the while, I wondered what tomorrow would bring.

Spending any length of time with Wade was downright terrifying.

CHAPTER 6

My alone time is for everyone's safety.

-Coffee Cup

Wade

"Seriously, what the fuck did I ever do to deserve this kind of life?" I groaned.

Seeing Landry standing on her porch in her tiny-ass fucking shorts had my cock hardening beyond anything that would ever be comfortable for a four-hour car ride.

Not to mention I was in pain on top of that, and in a really god-awful mood.

I was rethinking my ability to spend four hours in a vehicle with my ex-wife who still had the capability to bring me from soft to fully hard with just a goddamn look, especially dressed like she was.

"Fuckkk," I growled as I watched her walk down toward me. "Fuck my life."

I got out after I parked and walked around the car, limping only slightly as I opened her car door wide.

She smiled timidly at me and scooted around the car door, giving me a perfect view of her cleavage as she did.

Where the shorts were tight, the tank top was loose and flowy, showing off her impressive rack.

God, I loved her tits.

Loved and missed them.

"So, do you have any idea what's going on?" she asked. "Or is this just a joy ride?"

I snorted. "If it was a joy ride, I'd be on my bike. And as for what's going on, I got a call from my dad, who got a call from our lawyer. He needs to see us."

She gave me an assessing look, then dropped down into the car.

When her feet were in, I closed the door and tried not to show how much it hurt to walk as I moved back around the front of the car. Who was I kidding? I couldn't ride my bike that far with the kind of pain I was currently in.

Once I was in my seat again, the throbbing in my upper thigh simmered back down to manageable levels instead of gut boiling I'm-about-to-die pain.

"I seriously don't understand why the lawyer needs both of us present," Landry grumbled as she settled into her chair. "Or what would require us to be present at all."

Her skin stuck to the leather, and it made a farting sound, causing her to blush.

"That was the seat," she automatically replied.

I snorted. "Sure, it was."

Her face colored even darker. "I swear to God it was, Wade."

Inwardly I smiled.

Outwardly, I remained cool and collected.

This had always been the easy part between Landry and me, the back and forth banter that had was a part of how we communicated.

I loved this Landry.

It was the Landry who broke my heart, the one who left me, that I wasn't sure about.

She scooted again, trying to recreate the sound, and couldn't.

"Oh my God." She groaned. "Seriously."

I began to chuckle then.

Seeing her so flustered as she tried to recreate the sound had my belly loosening for the first time since yesterday when my dad had called me.

"I don't know why he needs us both there," I admitted. "But my dad called and said that the lawyer needed to talk to both of us, and he wouldn't say why. Swear to God."

She sighed. "At least it's not me driving."

I snorted. "When did you ever drive anywhere when I was in the car with you?"

She shrugged. "It's not like that anymore. I have to drive everywhere. I hate driving."

I barely refrained from saying, "Whose fault is that?"

Instead, I went with, "Well, I may have a bum leg that could give out on me in a couple of weeks, but for now it presses the gas pedal just fine."

She didn't say anything to that at first, only looked down at my affected leg.

"I can't feel my hand," she admitted. "At least, I can't most of the time. They said it was normal. Apparently, nerves were severed there, and it's possible I'll never fully regain complete control of it again."

The thought of Landry being hurt at all felt like a sucker punch straight to the sternum. It'd been a few weeks since it'd happened, and I still woke up in a sweat about it at night.

It'd happened because of what I'd been investigating. Jesus Christ, but had she not been there because of me, she would've been just fine right now instead of telling me in a shattered voice that her hand was numb.

"My doctors are worried about a bone infection," I admitted, unsure what to say to make this all better. "I've been on over four antibiotics now. If the one I'm on now doesn't kick my white blood cell count down, they're going to readmit me and drip some more IV antibiotics. Stronger ones that'll hopefully kick the infection's ass. Though, I hope the one I'm on now will do that."

"What if it doesn't?" she asked worriedly.

I swallowed hard, not ready to admit it even to myself what would happen.

But, like always, I didn't lie to Landry. I also didn't scale the truth to save her feelings.

"They might have to amputate my leg."

We were silent a while after that, digesting the impact of the words that had just come out of my mouth.

I'd just merged onto the highway when I looked over to find her tapping her fingers on her knees.

I barely smothered a grin.

Landry didn't like merging onto the highway. Never had, and I doubted ever would. When she drove, she avoided the highway altogether. It was only with me that she felt safe enough to go on it at all.

And, to prick her temper and get her mind off of what we were doing, I teased her.

Just like I always did.

"You missed a spot shaving," I pointed to her leg, right at the side of her knee.

She lifted said leg and said, "Where?"

I pointed it out again, this time touching her, and she groaned. "Holy shit. That's long!"

I rolled my eyes.

It wasn't that long, but it was a spot that she always missed for some reason. And since her leg hair was blonde, it was easy to miss.

As long as you weren't so in tune to a pair of legs like I was. Infatuation didn't even begin to cover it.

God, I missed everything about Landry.

Her sweet legs, and her long hair. Waking up to find her curled around me, stealing every single cover there was to have. Her taking such long showers that I was forced to take five-minute ones or risk having to take the remainder of it with cold water.

Hell, I even missed the bad.

The crying during at random times. The agonizing way she'd tear herself down. The way sometimes she'd go into one of these moods and not come out of it for a couple of days.

I now understood some of that to be the depression that Kourt had explained to me. It all made sense.

I wished I could go back in time.

I wished that I could make things right.

I wished that I hadn't tried to make her feel bad for not doing what I thought was the right thing when it came to donating to her sister.

Had I known then what I knew now, I wouldn't have said a word.

If I'd only left it alone…

"What are you doing?" I asked in confusion.

She pulled out a mini bottle of lotion, and then a small pink razor.

"I'm going to take care of this little patch," she murmured like I was dumb. "That okay?"

And before she'd even heard my reply, she applied the lotion and started to shave. In the front seat of my truck.

"What are you going to do with that?" I asked, eyeing the lotion and hair.

She pursed her lip and then eyed the window. "You fling that out of my window and it's going to go all down the side. I just had the truck washed."

She rolled her eyes. "I'll just put it in the bag in my purse," she murmured, doing just that.

Moments later, she sat back, and I had to smell the scent of her peaches and cream lotion for the next few miles and did so without saying a word.

It took me back to a time right after our first date.

And an idea struck me like a hammer coming down at the perfect angle on a nail's head.

Whack.

I'd remind her why we were good together.

Now that I had confirmation that her roommate was nothing more than a friend who supported her in her times of need, I realized rather quickly that the only reason I'd been staying away, giving her her space, was due to the fact that I had assumed that she had moved on with someone else.

Except she hadn't moved on, not even a little bit.

A person who's moved on doesn't get that upset over her ex-husband being hurt.

It just didn't happen.

For instance, if you were to ask Castiel, another club brother, what his ex-wife—who had divorced him because he was married to his job—would do if he'd been shot, it was not go to the hospital and wait for hours and hours. It was not, after getting shot in the hand after waiting those hours and hours, sit in an uncomfortable plastic chair beside your ex-husband's bedside.

What Castiel's ex-wife would have done was to receive the phone call, hang up the phone, and then celebrate that she was finally rid of him.

That was not Landry.

Landry cared, but I could tell that my job scared the crap out of her.

Yet, even despite her worry over my occupation, she fully supported me.

I shifted, my leg starting to throb, and Landry's eyes once again came to me.

"Can I ask you a hypothetical question without you getting upset?" She tilted her head warily in my direction.

I knew what she was going to ask. She wanted to know what I'd do without my leg.

"I guess," I acquiesced.

"If you have to have your leg amputated, will you still be able to ride a motorcycle?" she questioned.

I felt my stomach somersault.

"The infection is down by my knee for some reason. It's my hope that I don't have to have it amputated, but they said that if it was needed, then it would be an above-the-knee amputation. It will depend on where, exactly, they perform the amputation that would answer that question better. I would think that as long as I still have a stump to attach a prosthesis to, then it should be okay." I paused, thinking about something else. "I don't know if I'll be able to run."

She looked at me with sadness filling her features.

Running had always been my escape.

I was a big man, tall at six-foot-four-inches, and I had long legs that allowed me to eat up the ground. When I needed a break from reality, I slid on a pair of running shoes and let the burn of my muscles take me away for a while.

But, if my leg was gone, would that even be possible anymore?

"There are amputee runners all over the world," she disagreed with me. "There's a cop on the Kilgore SWAT team that just ran a marathon. It was a big deal. The Old Dogs New Tricks Rescue sponsored him."

I felt fondness at hearing Landry had sponsored him.

When we'd first gotten together, Landry had fallen in love with an old dog at a shelter the day we'd gone there to find a puppy so Butters, my old Labrador, could have a playmate.

We'd left with a dog, of course, but not a young one. An older one that was well on his way to death.

But, Landry had wanted that dog, and we'd gotten him.

He'd passed away peacefully in his sleep about six months after we'd gotten him, and that had started her love for older rescue dogs. She'd started up a dog rescue, and now went around to shelters and found every older dog that was being passed over by prospective new dog owners. Dogs that were ugly and just wouldn't be able to pull off the 'cute' card. Dogs that were handicapped. Dogs that were temperamental. She found them homes.

My plan to remind her of all the good we had firmly in my mind, I took the next exit and pulled up outside a convenience store.

"Let's go grab something to eat that'll tide us over until lunchtime," I murmured.

She eyed me warily.

I knew what she was thinking.

I hated to stop, and I'd literally just offered to do so without her even asking me.

What was my game plan?

I could practically hear her wheels spinning, and I wanted to laugh.

Instead of giving her any indication that I was up to something, I pushed the car door open and got out, smiling when she stayed put until I could make my way around the car.

Old habits die hard, and Landry and I had it out quite a few times in the beginning of our relationship. After realizing that opening the door for her wasn't going to cause any unwanted side effects on her end, she gave in and allowed me to open her car door for her like I wanted to, and I did it from that point on.

I was happy to see that she allowed me to do it today.

"Thanks," I murmured as I opened first her car door, and then the door to the convenience store. "I was hoping you wouldn't give me shit."

She snorted. "I lost that battle a long time ago, Wade. And, if it makes you happy to open the car door for me, who am I to tell you that you can't?"

I winked at her and went down the aisle that had the beef jerky, while she went to the one that had the candy.

I stepped wrong when I bent down to get my favorite brand and felt bile rise up my throat as my wound reminded me that it hated me for only the seventy-fifth time today.

"Wade?"

I dropped my eyes so she wouldn't see the pain, and said, "Yeah?"

"You want me to get it?" she offered.

No. What I wanted was for my leg to be better. What I wanted was for her to be back in my bed. What I wanted was for my life to be what it was before she'd left.

What I got wasn't that.

But I was working on it.

"Yeah," I croaked. "Would you?"

She bent down and the tank she was wearing rode up, displaying a sliver of skin above her shorts.

My tattoo was on her upper hip, right where I'd left it.

It was a picture of a shield—my badge—and my numbers on it.

She'd gotten it the day before we'd married, and then had shown it to me the moment we'd arrived in Bora Bora for our honeymoon.

I'd fucked her…

I immediately shut that line of thought off before I could so much as think about how it felt to be inside of her while staring at my stamp on her right hip.

If I didn't, I'd not only have a stiff, sore leg, but I'd also wind up with a stiff, throbbing cock.

"Thank you," I murmured when she stood up, her shirt once again covering her tattoo.

She smiled at me. "I got what I want. I'm going to go to the bathroom just in case, and I'll meet you at the door."

I grinned.

She knew I wouldn't leave her in here alone.

I'd never been able to do that—walk out and wait in the car.

It was an odd habit that my father had also done for my mother and sisters. I'd done it for my sisters, and then Landry.

God, I missed her.

I missed her so bad that it hurt.

"Okay, honey." I lifted my hand as if to touch her cheek, and her eyes widened.

I stopped short of actually touching her, realizing what I was doing almost too late, and let my hand drop. "Sorry.

She smiled and patted my hand, then walked away, once again leaving me to stare at her ass the entire way.

Lani Lynn Vale

CHAPTER 7

You look like something I drew with my left hand.

-Text from Wade to Landry

Landry

I felt like I was struggling to breathe.

God.

How had he known that I needed to stop? How had he known that I was hungry?

Why did the man know me so well?

At least, well enough to know my signs, I supposed.

After washing my hands in the sink, I dried them and contemplated how the next couple of hours were going to go.

I had a feeling not very good based on the way my heart was racing, and my knees felt weak.

Pushing through, though, I made my way outside to see him standing at the entrance of the building, waiting on me like he always did.

I smiled.

That smile grew even wider when I saw him clock the woman holding the screaming baby, looking extremely flummoxed as she tried to calm the baby down.

She had a toddler at her hip, whom she was holding onto by his shoulder with her one free hand, and she was watching another child get her own Icee, and making a big damn mess while doing it.

"No, honey," the mother was trying to explain. "Put the lid on first."

I continued to watch as Wade limped his way over, trying to conceal his pain the entire way.

When he arrived at the Icee machine, he helped the kid get the lid on the cup, then handed it back to her.

The kid, who had to be about four or five, looked over at Wade and grinned.

Kids always loved Wade. Always.

I didn't know why. I didn't know how. But I'd never seen one child who was afraid of him. Which usually ended up freaking the parent out.

"Thank you," the mother said. "She's independent and wanted to do it herself but as you can see she's just not there yet."

The mother lifted her hand from the toddler to gesture at her other child, and the toddler took off.

It was then I realized the reason behind the grip on the toddler.

He was a runner.

Wade caught him before he could skirt by him to the rack of candy at Wade's back and picked him up in his arms.

"No!" the toddler yelled.

I tensed, wondering if the mother would take offense to Wade holding the kid.

Most did.

Wade was a big guy, and though he looked friendly, today he was wearing his motorcycle vest and that sometimes squigged parents out. When he was in his police officer uniform, it was fine.

But I shouldn't have worried. The woman didn't seem to care in the least that some random biker had just picked up her child.

Why did she not care? Because there was a man that was coming out of the bathroom who looked just as scary as Wade dressed in a cut just like Wade—only his deemed him a member of the Uncertain Saints.

"Yo," the man said as he sidled up to us. "Need help, Mama?"

"Ridley," the woman sighed. "Jesus, I didn't think you were ever going to finish."

He shrugged. "It's not like I can tell my shit to come out any faster than it was. Wade, what the fuck?"

Wade, who obviously knew this Ridley person, handed him his kid in a smooth transfer then offered his hand to him.

Ridley took both, settling the toddler on his hip before taking Wade's hand.

"Ridley," Wade said. "It's nice to see you. What are you doing in these parts?"

"Taking a shit," he answered bluntly.

Wade grunted a response. "That's not what I meant, and you know it."

The woman who belonged with Ridley handed the baby over to Ridley as well and then went to help her other child get a straw for the Icee. Ridley automatically curled his arm around the baby and started to bounce him. The baby didn't like that any more than just being held.

"I'm on a seventeen-hour road trip to goddamn Disney World." He paused. "We're only on hour two, and I'm having a hard time staying sane. I'm not sure why the fuck we're all going to Disney, but whatever. I'm fairly sure I should've objected. I would have had I known this one was going to scream for the entire trip."

I snickered, causing Ridley and Wade to both look at me.

Ridley's eyes were dark and knowing as he said, "Friend of yours, Wade?"

"Wife," Wade answered immediately, then winced. "Ex-wife."

"Huh," Ridley replied.

The kid changed to another decibel and I walked over and smiled at Ridley as I said, "May I?"

Ridley shrugged and handed the baby over.

Though I may not have any kids of my own, I had run a daycare for the last few years. I dealt with babies all day, every day. They were my favorite part of working there.

Wade's eyes warmed as he looked at me with the baby, and I turned my face away to look at the screaming infant.

"Shhhh," I whispered into the baby's ear, shushing and rocking.

Pulling the blankie closer around the baby, I turned him slightly in so that he was secure, and then hummed to him.

It didn't take long, but what Wade had called Landry's Secret Shake and Shush started to work. The baby's wails turned to hiccups and then relaxed even further into complete sleep.

"Well, it's official," Ridley's wife said. "We'll have to take her to Disney with us."

I looked at the woman and grinned. "Don't feel bad. I do this all day every day. I have a daycare with about eight babies in it right now. When I'm not in the office, I'm in there helping calm the little ones. We have four babies under eight weeks, and two under six months. The older two are ten and eleven months, but they were there from the beginning, too. I do this way too much not to be good at it."

She smiled at me in return. "My name is Freya, and if you ever want to leave your job and become my nanny, I'll pay you in Hershey kisses and stray lasagna noodles."

I burst out laughing, causing the baby's eyes to open.

But the baby didn't start screaming.

Instead, he started to look around expectantly. Then let out a rather large belch.

"Kid's gassy as fuck," Ridley grunted. "And I still have fifteen more hours of this bullshit."

Freya smacked her husband on the ass and said, "You wanted the third. I specifically remember you telling me that it'd be perfectly fine. That third babies were always the easiest. Well, you were wrong."

My lips quirked.

Ridley took his wife by the nape of the neck and pulled her into him, causing me to look away.

Right into a pair of eyes that looked like they were on fire.

I tilted my head and stared at Wade.

"What?" I asked, feeling my heart start to race.

He looked down at the child in my arms, and then back at me. "Nothing."

His rumbled words may have come off nonchalant, but they weren't.

I knew Wade.

He was thinking something about me, and it was making him hard.

I felt myself squirm, then walked over to the parents that were not through with their kisses and deposited their kid into Freya's arms.

"It's all in the shush," I told her, trying valiantly to avoid the practical sear of heat coming off of Wade. "Sometimes you have to do it loud enough so they can hear it over their own cries, but I swear to Christ it works."

Freya took her bundled son who was now staring around like it was all a party and grinned at me.

"I'll give it a try." She smiled.

Then her toddler knocked the Icee out of the other child's hands, and red slush went everywhere.

Ridley sighed. "I'm sure you're thankful you don't have kids right about now."

That was directed at Wade, who was staring at the mess on the floor like it only amused him.

"I'd give my right leg to have a kid of my own, Ridley," Wade said, breaking my heart all over again.

And there was the other reason I'd left.

I couldn't have kids.

One infection after a donation I'd given had left me infertile. So, I would never be having kids of my own—or giving Wade any of his.

Not only had the infection fried my reproductive system, but they'd taken my ovaries with the infection. To put the icing on the cake, I'd learned at the age of fifteen that my parents really didn't care at all about me, because instead of trying to save my reproductive organs, my parents took the easy way out and just had them removed in case things went wrong in the future.

Why?

Because what if I got too sick, and couldn't give their favorite daughter bone marrow if she may need it?

I'd, of course, known that my parents were pieces of shits from a very young age, but I hadn't realized how far they'd stoop until they'd taken a piece of me that I hadn't realized that I wanted until it was gone.

I felt something like a lead weight settle in my stomach, and I smiled at the crowd that was now gathered around.

"You ready, Wade?" I asked softly.

Wade's gaze met mine, and I saw something there that was really close to understanding.

Wade had seen my reaction and didn't understand it.

But he'd try to figure out why, and I had a feeling I wasn't going to like the conversation that followed if he did find out.

But at this point, if he asked, I just might tell him what was wrong.

Which was exactly what he did the moment we got back into the car.

And, still feeling the heat emanating from the man beside me, I decided that it didn't matter.

So what, if he knew why I was so sad?

"What's wrong?" he asked. "Why did you get such a long face when I said I wanted kids?"

I laughed softly under my breath.

"I'm sad because I want kids, too," I told him truthfully. "It makes me sad that I can't have them."

He was silent for a few long seconds.

"We could have them," he said, sounding as if he was gentling a skittish horse. "If you wanted to."

I laughed, and that laugh turned into a sniffle as the tears started to prickle my eyes. "If it was only that easy."

He shifted into fourth gear as he started to merge onto the freeway, and my breath caught like it always did as we rushed into traffic at breakneck speeds.

I closed my eyes and breathed through the terror.

"It's that easy if we make it that easy," he said, sounding confident. "We could share them."

I swallowed past a lump in my throat. "If it were possible to have kids on my end, Wade, I might very well take you up on that offer. But I can't. I had that possibility ripped away from me at fifteen."

Understanding dawned in his eyes, and I felt the lowest of lows at seeing the look there.

"When we met, you said you didn't want kids. You made it very clear before we married that you didn't." He paused. "You lied. You want kids, you just can't have them."

I nodded. "Correct."

"Explains the no period thing…" He frowned. "Why lie about that?"

I looked down at my hands. "Because I hate thinking about it? Because had I told you that I couldn't have kids, I would've then had to go into detail about *why* I couldn't have kids. About how I donated bone marrow to my sister against my will, and that I got an infection that spread to my reproductive organs, which then were taken out of me instead of trying to correct the infection with antibiotics."

Wade's free hand clenched into a tight fist, while his hand on the steering wheel tightened until his knuckles were white.

"You're saying they just took them out instead of fighting with antibiotics?" he clarified.

I thought about that for a second. "They tried antibiotics. But, unlike with you, they didn't keep on top of them. I just kept getting sicker and sicker until the infection had spread to my fallopian tubes. Taking my ovaries was precautionary, however."

He blew out a breath. "If I'd known…"

I shrugged. "If you'd known, you wouldn't have done anything differently because you're not the type of person that would leave a person like Lina hurting if you didn't have to."

I was, though.

I would have…had Wade not made me see things I didn't wish to see.

Kind of like the day he'd found out about Lina, and how he'd encouraged me to donate to her because I wouldn't be able to live with myself if she died.

He was right.

As much as I hated donating to her, I'd still do it if she absolutely needed it. Regardless of my feelings toward her, she was still my sister.

Even if my sister hated me.

"Can you open my sunflower seeds?" he asked, gesturing to the unopened bag that was still in the large sack that held the rest of our food.

I picked the sack up and reached inside, smiling widely when I saw the Snickers bar.

"This yours?" I asked.

He rolled his eyes. "No. Yours. You know I don't like caramel."

I did know that.

I also knew that he hated the smell most, and it got to the point where I couldn't even eat the Snickers in front of him because he could smell the caramel.

I was fairly sure he was full of shit, but that argument was so old that I'd gotten to the point where I just did what he asked because it was easier than listening to him moan and whine for an hour.

But, since I loved Snickers so much, I still ate them. I was just hyperaware of where I ate them and brushed my teeth immediately afterward.

"You're going to let me eat it in front of you?" I asked, spotting the second one underneath his seeds—which I opened for him and handed over.

He took the bag and reached inside, pulling out a small handful which immediately went into his mouth.

He sucked them all to one side and then reached for the cup that was in the center console. An Icee one that he'd stolen from the gas station.

I'd always been curious about how he held so much in his mouth while also opening the seeds with his teeth and tongue. Then there was the fact that he could also talk and hold conversations while he had his mouth full.

"Why are you looking at me like that?" he questioned.

I smiled. "You know I'm watching you and trying to figure out how you're opening those while you have a mouthful of seeds, and you're still talking to me."

He spat an empty shell out into the cup and looked at me. "I'm just talented. What can I say?"

I rolled my eyes.

Though, Wade did have a point.

He was very talented with his mouth. I knew that firsthand.

On our first date, he'd tied a cherry stem with only his tongue, and had given it to me by way of his mouth kissing mine.

My eyes had widened when he'd transferred that knotted stem into my mouth by way of his tongue sneaking in.

I had melted right then and there, and the memory still made me hot as hell.

"What was that look for?" he asked.

I bit my lip and looked away. "Well," I hesitated. Did I really want to tell him what that memory was for? Then I decided, why the hell not? "I was thinking about our first date and the cherry stem you tied into a knot with your tongue."

His lips quirked up at one side. "I remember that. Vividly."

I flushed hotly and turned my head down to my lap. Then I busied myself with searching through the mountain of snacks we'd gotten at the convenience store.

"How did you know that couple and their kids?" I wondered, choosing a bag of corn nuts and ripping into them.

"Ridley is a biker. Bikers know the bikers in their area, though Uncertain is a little far from Bear Bottom. We do run into each other a time or two during the year. We mainly know each other from the Toy Runs we run each year right before Christmas. About six or seven clubs from the surrounding three states meet up and make a run. All the donations we collect and toys go to children in need," he explained.

I nodded my head in understanding. "Gotcha. I liked that run."

I went on that run once and only once, but it was my first big run that I'd ever gone on with Wade on the bike in front of me.

"The one this year is going to be good," he said. "We're going to have ten clubs participating, and we're sponsoring the Children's Hospital in Dallas. All those kids that are there for various reasons will have their entire Christmas covered."

That made my heart swell.

"You did that because of Rome's son, didn't you?" I asked softly.

Wade shrugged. "It was a suggestion, yes. But Rome was the one to really start planning it out. Him and his new old lady, Izzy."

Rome, one of Wade's MC brothers, had a son who had died of Leukemia. I'd met Izzy once, but since I was no longer a part of the MC life since I'd divorced Wade, I hadn't seen any reason to become friendly with her. The moment she'd realized who I was, she'd been standoffish. Everybody always was once they learned who I was, and who I was no longer married to.

Speaking of which. "Bayou actually talked to me yesterday like I was a normal human being. Do you happen to know why?"

Wade snorted. "You are a normal human being, Landry."

I narrowed my eyes. "Did you say something to him?"

Wade shook his head. "No."

I tilted my head slightly to the side and stuffed some corn nuts into my open mouth to keep myself from calling him a liar.

"Why do you eat those?" he suddenly burst out. "They're so gross."

They weren't gross.

"Why are you such a weenie when it comes to smells?" I asked. "You bought this Snickers knowing you weren't going to like the smell of me eating it in this closed cab. Which, by the way, you hate me doing anyway. Why are you being so nice all of a sudden?"

Wade shrugged. "A lot of things have changed. Things that used to bug me no longer do."

"Why?" I pushed.

He turned his blinker on and went around a car, causing my heart to accelerate because he'd cut off a big black truck to do it, and then said, "Do you want the truth?"

I nodded. "I always want the truth from you."

He moved back over to the slow lane, and the big black truck flipped him off as he flew past.

Wade flipped him right back off himself, and then bit the corner of his mouth as he began thinking.

Likely wondering whether he should really tell me the truth or not.

"Because," he paused. "When you left, I realized those petty little stupid things we fought over were just that—stupid. In the grand scheme of things, I'd rather deal with all those things that used to bother the hell out of me if it only meant you were back at my side still doing them."

I didn't know what to say to that.

"I hate what happened between us."

I felt my heart skip a beat at his exclamation.

"I hate that it happened, and I hate that you had to go through your childhood like you did. We were so good together. You took you away from me, and even after all this time apart, I still don't know how to function without you."

I swallowed hard, wondering what in the hell I was supposed to say to that.

"Wade…"

"I shouldn't have forced you to do something you didn't want to do," he said. "I should have taken what you said to heart. I should've let you do what you wanted, and I should have supported you in every decision that you made, regardless of whether I agreed with it or not. Because that is part of what being married is about, compromise and understanding. I wasn't either of those things and by not supporting you in your decision, I ruined our lives."

How long had I wanted to hear that?

"Wade…"

"And then it all starts making a sick sort of sense when you said today that you couldn't have kids," he continued. "That morning, before your sister had come, I told you that I wanted a child and you'd shut down."

I had.

As luck would have it, my sister had come over right after that argument had taken place and told me that she needed another bone marrow transplant. It'd been perfect timing, really.

"You didn't just leave me because of what happened with your sister, did you?"

No, I hadn't.

"You wouldn't have stopped wanting them," I said softly.

He growled. "Did you ever stop to consider that there were alternate ways of having a child that didn't include you conceiving and carrying it?"

I looked away.

Yes, I'd considered that.

And I'd even thought to mention it…but then my sister had shown, and Wade had literally torn my heart out for a second time that day and I'd…reacted.

It hadn't been a good reaction.

In fact, I wasn't proud of what I'd done. I should've done things a hell of a lot differently than I had. Yet, I couldn't make myself.

"I have depression issues," I finally admitted. "And honestly, even if there was another way to have children, I'm not the right person to be raising them. Not with all the shit that goes on in my head."

He growled in frustration. "You'll just use anything as an excuse, won't you?"

I frowned and snapped my gaze to his. "What? No!"

"We were married for almost a year and a half, and since we've been divorced, I've had time to think about our time together. You want to know something?" He didn't wait for me to answer him with a yes or a no. "I think that you always had one foot out the door. You were always ready, just waiting for me to screw up. I think I scared you by asking you to marry me, and you were so fuckin' happy that you said yes without thinking it through."

I frowned. "What are you talking about?"

"You were always waiting for the other shoe to drop," he explained. "You were waiting for me to find something to hate you for, so instead of waiting for me to find it, you found something that was big enough—a good enough reason—to leave *me* for."

I opened my mouth to deny it, to tell him that he was so full of crap it was coming out of his ears, and promptly shut my mouth.

Because…he was right.

And I had absolutely nothing to say to it.

The next few minutes I sat completely stock still in my chair, my heart racing, as I tried to come up with something to say that would refute what he'd just said…but nothing ever came to my lips.

"I think you wait for me to treat you like your parents treat you," he rumbled quietly. "And honey, I'm not your parents."

I reached into the bag that was now between my feet, and took out the Snickers, opening it and shoving a large bite in my mouth before chewing it quickly. Then another. And another.

When I was done with the entire bar, I reached for the other Snickers.

That was gone in less than two miles, too.

"I love…" he started, and I screamed.

"Don't!"

He continued speaking. "…you."

I shook my head fast and hard. "No!"

"I love you," he repeated again.

I shook my head against my headrest. "Please stop."

"I have loved you from the moment I first saw you," he continued.

I shook my head and closed my eyes. "Please stop. Please."

"I love you. I love you. I love you," he repeated.

I started to hyperventilate.

"Nothing you can do or say can change how I feel." He pushed, "I've been yours from the moment you walked into my classroom and gave me your eyes."

I swallowed hard.

"Wade, please," I whispered. "You don't know what you're getting into."

How About No

He snorted. "I know exactly what I'm getting into."

I shook my head, frantically trying to come up with something that would stop this.

"No, you don't," I argued. "You don't know anything."

That's when he laughed.

Wade? He had a great laugh. It'd always made me weak in the knees, and I hadn't heard it for so long that I wasn't prepared for it.

I wasn't prepared for the way he threw his head back and let his amusement loose.

Because, maybe if I had been, I wouldn't have been watching him at the time. I wouldn't have been so caught up in the wonder that I couldn't look away.

Hell, even the fact that he'd taken his eyes off the road didn't affect me—even though it should have.

He started laughing so hard that tears came to his eyes.

And when he finally stopped, returning his eyes to the road, I still stared.

"I know you," he said on a small laugh. "I know you better than I know anyone."

I shook my head in denial.

Then I tried the last thing I ever wanted to try—but I needed him to stop. He had to move on with his life – without me.

Because I wasn't capable of leaving Wade a second time.

And I had a feeling if I didn't dissuade him soon, then he'd be back in my life, and I wouldn't have anything to stop him with.

"I'm sleeping with Kourt," I lied. "I've been sleeping with Kourt since before you even came in the picture."

And, out of all the things I expected him to do, I didn't expect him to take my hand and tell me what he told me next.

"You're so full of shit it's coming out of your ears. You're not sleeping with anyone, and you haven't since we split. You can keep Kourt in your life, honey," he told me. "You can keep your best friend while I'm with you. But, just sayin', you and I are going to happen. You don't have to lie about sleeping with your best friend, because you don't get a choice in the matter anymore. I'm going to make it work between us, and you're going to let me do it because you don't have a choice."

"I've had suicidal thoughts."

All amusement fled his face.

"I know," he murmured, his voice soft. "And it hurts my heart that it got to that point for you and that it was a defining moment in your life. If you hadn't done that, you might've never become such good friends with Kourt. In turn, you might've never moved here, and I might not have met you."

I swallowed hard.

I'd just told him my most painful, personal secret, and he'd…accepted it.

"How do you know?" I whispered.

I was almost afraid to ask.

But, I had to know.

Was it my parents? My sister?

Though, I wouldn't think that either of them would care enough to tell on me. They were selfish beings. They didn't care about my life, as long as I was there to be used when they needed to use me.

"Kourt."

All the breath was ripped out of my chest.

"Kourt?" I croaked, stunned.

Wade nodded, calmly going around a slower moving car. "Kourt."

I opened my mouth, then closed it.

"W-when?" I stuttered.

"The day I was shot," he answered simply. "I would've come after you then, but I was kind of, sort of, maybe too weak to do it. Plus, I had some anger to work through. I wanted to be able to come to you, to talk to you, without wanting to wring your damn neck."

I looked down at my hands and clenched them, then leaned forward and started to sift through the bag of food.

There was nothing else to eat but a couple of protein bars that Wade had bought, and there was no way in hell I was touching those.

They were disgusting.

I'd tried them once when I was hungry, and had tasted the disgusting things in my mouth for a half a day afterward.

"You don't have to be mad at your friend, baby," he said to me. "He was only looking out for you."

I knew that.

That didn't make my heart feel better, though.

My best friend had shared my dirty little secrets, and there was nothing I could do about it.

I felt utterly betrayed.

"I'll never marry you again," I whispered.

He patted my hand. "As long as I have you, I don't care if we're married." He paused. "But, just sayin', I'm not going to settle for anything less than everything from you. One day, I'll convince you."

The fact that he sounded so sure of himself made me want to punch him.

But I didn't say a word. Not for the next two hours. Not after my final parting comment.

"You know how badly you wanted to take my ass and I never let you?" I whispered furiously. "Well, this is also something that you're not going to get."

CHAPTER 8

It's not about how many times you fall. It's how many times you get back up.

-Wade listening to a DWI suspect

Wade

"Do you want me to stop?" I asked Landry.

She shook her head.

The last two hours had been filled with enough silence that it would've bothered another man.

It didn't bother me.

When Landry was pissed, and she knew she was right, she'd talk until she was blue in the face.

But, over the last couple of hours, she'd had absolutely nothing to say to refute my earlier words. Words that I'd meant every single one of.

I didn't care if we were divorced.

I didn't care if she thought that our being together was a lost cause.

I was going to make us work, even if I had to do all the work myself.

I'd failed her by not listening to her, not trying to figure out why she hadn't wanted to donate her bone marrow. I had pressured her to the point that she felt like she had no other choice than to leave me. I wouldn't fail her again.

I'd fight until there was nothing left of me.

"Well then, I guess we'll head straight to the lawyer's office. Sound good to you?" I asked.

Landry sighed. "Sure."

Lips twitching, I passed all of the restaurants in town and headed downtown straight to the lawyer's office that we used—I had no clue why we didn't use one closer, but I hadn't known any lawyers except for the one my dad had used.

Since we had no children and I gave her everything, Landry had drawn up divorce papers online. I'd gone along with her. We had the final decrees sent to my uncle Jimmy, also my dad's lawyer after it was drawn up.

I had never used a lawyer for anything but that divorce in my whole life. Now I was regretting that because I should've found someone closer. Certainly closer than four hours.

And I wished that I had never had to use a lawyer at all. There was that.

Arriving downtown, I sighed when I didn't see any parking spaces that were big enough.

"You're going to have to park in BFE," she murmured.

Bum-fuck-Egypt.

I rolled my eyes and did just that, not caring in the least until I got out of the truck and realized that I was going to have to walk three blocks to get where I needed to go.

She saw my hesitation as I rounded her side of the truck and opened her door for her.

"Do you want me to drop you off?" she offered.

I snorted and held out my hand, which she took.

The feel of her tiny, soft hand in my big, rough one made my heart hammer.

Something so small shouldn't make such a big hole in my heart, should it?

But it did.

There was so much I missed.

Holding her hand. Brushing the hair back off her face. Pulling her body in tight to mine. Pressing myself up against her ass as she bent over the sink to brush her teeth. The way she used to leave her long hair on the shower glass.

Hell, I even missed the way she swore up and down that she didn't fart.

The girl was so adamant that she didn't do anything of the sort that it was comical.

According to her, she was God's one exception to the rule. She did not do those kinds of things—even though we both knew she did.

Hell, I swore on all that was holy that the girl got up an hour early just so she could do the things—such as taking a shit—that she was just too embarrassed to do when I was around or awake.

"Are you coming?" she asked, looking at me weirdly.

But she didn't take her hand away.

And I was reluctant to let it go, even though I wanted to.

"Landry!"

I turned just as my mother came barreling toward us, pushing me aside.

I stepped back from Landry and dropped her hand, only for my leg to nearly give out from underneath me.

I felt bile rise up my throat, and it took everything that I had not to bend over and throw up right then and there.

I should've been better by now.

I shouldn't hurt this much so long after I'd been shot.

Yet, I did hurt.

Obviously, I knew it wasn't going to heal in a day, but it should be at least a little bit better by this point.

But it wasn't.

And I had a feeling, one deep in my gut, that this wound was not a simple one. It wasn't going to be fixed…and I was likely going to lose my leg.

Speaking of which, I drew a deep steadying breath and reached past Landry, who was in my mother's arms and got my bottle of pills. Popping them open, I threw one of the horse pill antibiotics in my mouth and swallowed it dry.

It stuck in my throat about halfway down, and I reached for Landry's drink that she'd yet to finish.

Washing it down the rest of the way, I licked my lips and tasted her apple Chapstick, groaning at the flavor.

God, I'd loved it when I kissed her and tasted that.

It was so perfectly her.

"Oh, I've missed you," my mother said, pulling back.

"You haven't missed me?" I croaked.

My mother glanced at me, stuck out her tongue, and then pulled Landry in for one more quick hug.

"I've missed you, too," she said, her eyes turning to concern. "Are you okay?"

Landry's eyes went to me, and her frown deepened.

"What's wrong?" she asked, pulling away and moving toward me.

Oh, nothing much. I think my leg is about to fall off due to the pain I'm in.

"Stepped wrong," I lied.

"Stepped wrong my ass," my father grunted as he finally caught up to my mother, who had obviously run ahead of him. "You pushed him out of the way, and he had to stumble to catch his balance. You're lucky the truck was right there, or he would've fallen straight on his ass. Jesus, Minnie. He was just shot not long ago!" my father, Porter, growled. "And you. You went and got yourself shot, too. What the fuck is going on in Texas?"

Landry smiled at my father, and tears came to her eyes.

The minute my dad saw that, he sighed and said, "Come 'ere, girl."

Landry threw herself at my old man, and I felt my heart skip a beat inside my chest.

Not only had she left me, but she'd left my family too.

My parents had adored her from the moment that they'd met her, and Landry had latched onto them like they would leave her at any second.

My dad reached around Landry's body to wrap her up tight and narrowly missed smacking me in the face as he did.

"You're talking about me not paying attention," my mother, Minnie, laughed. "You almost clocked him in the face!"

Porter shrugged, uncaring. "Sometimes you gotta do what you gotta do."

I rolled my eyes and took a step away from the truck in the direction of my mother.

My mom wrapped her arms around me gently and said, "You okay?"

I nodded and dropped my mouth to the top of her head, inhaling the floral scent that she'd worn since I was a child, and feeling like I was home. "Yeah, Ma. I'm good. How are you?"

"I'd be good if that lawyer asshole would tell me what was going on," she muttered.

"That lawyer asshole is your brother," I paused. "And why wouldn't he tell you?"

Porter moved until his arm was across Landry's shoulders. "Let's go find out."

And that's what we did.

Arriving in the lawyer's office—my uncle Jimmy's office—I took a seat and nearly groaned audibly at the way the pressure was taken off of my leg.

"Fuck, that hurts," I growled, feeling my stomach clench, and my ears beginning to lose the slight ring.

"Got that right," my father muttered.

I looked over at my old man, who'd also taken his seat on the comfortable leather couch just down from me.

"Back acting up again?" I questioned.

He grunted. "Been acting up for the last thirty years."

I snorted. "If I keep this leg, I have a feeling that it's going to do the same damn thing."

"You'll feel it every single time the weather acts up," he promised.

I was not looking forward to that. Not even a little bit.

I'd been in the Army for three years as an MP—military police—before getting out and joining up with first Benton's police department, and then almost immediately moving to Bear Bottom PD.

Needless to say, those three years in the Army had not been kind to my joints. We still did quite a bit of patrolling while carrying gear in the military police. Some of the places we had to investigate in the Middle East would never be kind even to the healthiest of people. We investigated murders, missing soldiers, domestic violence, anything that might happen in the states, just in worse conditions.

Now, add on being shot in the thigh, and that wound not healing correctly…I had a feeling I was really fucked.

"Great," I muttered, closing my eyes.

The couch beside me depressed, and I didn't have to open my eyes to know that Landry had just taken the spot between me and my father. She was so close that I could feel the heat of her along my left side.

Everything inside of me urged me to throw my arm around her shoulder and pull her in close to my side.

I debated it for all of three seconds before I said "fuck it" in my head and did what I wanted.

Lifting my arm, I didn't bother trying to act smooth, as if pulling her into me was just something that happened.

Nope. I went ahead and wrapped my arm around her shoulders, cupped her elbow, and pulled her into my side.

At first, she stiffened, and I was sure that she was going to pull away.

But then she surprised the shit out of me by not only staying where I put her but also laying her head against my pectoral.

Everything inside of me soared.

Everything.

My heart raced. My hopes lifted. The throbbing in my leg faded into the background.

Hell, even my bladder that'd been protesting for the last hour had paled in comparison to how it felt to have her in my arms, back where she fucking belonged.

We stayed like that for thirty blissful seconds before my uncle Jimmy came out of his office and said, "All right, boys and girls. Y'all can come back now."

I grunted as Landry used my full bladder to push herself away from me, scooting to the edge of the couch and opened one eye to glare at the man.

He was grinning at me.

I silently curled my lip at him and flipped him off for good measure.

He shrugged.

"Can we have the meeting right here?" I requested. "I have to pee, my leg hurts, and if I have to get up again, it's not going to be good."

"Why don't you pee then?" Uncle Jimmy suggested. "There's this new modern invention called the toilet. You go in there, lift the lid because your aunt Martha will kick your ass if you pee on her seat, and then take a leak into the little porcelain bowl. It's great. You should try it."

I flipped him off again and closed my eyes once more.

"Because walking to the bathroom might very well make me throw up right now," I told him honestly. "My leg hurts really fuckin' bad."

Jimmy's face went soft. "We can do it out here," he agreed. "But I can't promise that my next client won't walk in during the middle of it."

"If that happens," I sighed. "Then we'll move. But until then, this couch has accepted me as one of its own for the time being."

Landry settled back into the couch but didn't move back into my side.

My parents, who'd been quiet up until this point, both started talking at once.

"So, let's get this shit over with. What's the deal?" my father asked at the same time my mother said, "Tell us already, please."

Jimmy walked over to the receptionist's desk, who wasn't anywhere to be seen, and rolled the chair over before sitting down in the middle of the waiting room.

It was then that I saw a stack of papers in his hands.

I frowned, the signature on the paper at the bottom looking achingly familiar.

It was our divorce papers.

Something inside of me perked up, and I clenched my hand as I repositioned myself so that I was now leaning forward.

"What?" I rushed out.

He looked at me, then moved his eyes to Landry, who was mimicking my pose.

"Well," he said, sounding worried. "I'll just go ahead and start, I guess. I got a call earlier this week from an FBI agent who said that he was calling about ninety lawyers to tell them the same thing that he was telling me."

"And that was..." I urged.

"That was to say that there was something wrong with a case that I was listed as a contact on. Apparently, they investigated over thirty-two Texas counties, and forty-one individuals working on the cases under question. The individuals being investigated were embezzling money from the cases they were working, and then either hiding the cases altogether in layers of red tape or sending out fake documents that proceedings were taken care of when they weren't." He paused for effect. "Over two thousand divorces that were pushed through these counties were null and void over the last eight years. Y'all's being one of them. For all intents and purposes, y'all are still officially married to each other."

Silence.

Nothing but silence.

Then Landry squeaked. "What? *How? I have papers saying that we are officially divorced!*"

"Well, apparently they just never filed them through an official court. They received payment, fabricated fake paperwork, and then sent it to the clients. You got the paperwork they sent you, yes, but the court—and judge's—signature was forged. And, that judge isn't actually a judge at all—just a clerk. You are not divorced. You're still legally married," Jimmy explained.

Something close to elation started to pour through me.

"How does that even work?" my mother asked. "That's absurd."

"It is," he agreed. "And the only reason it was found was because a couple was audited because they'd filed jointly for the last eighteen years, and then filed separately, both trying to claim their children. It was then discovered that they were officially still married even though they tried to explain that they weren't. Which then caused the FBI to get involved with their embezzlement unit. You're one of two thousand cases, and there is currently a class action lawsuit for this if you're interested in participating in it."

More silence followed.

"So...we're still married," I said, trying not to sound as excited as I felt.

"Yes." Uncle Jimmy nodded, reading me like an open book. "You are."

I looked over at Landry who was leaning forward and had her arms wrapped tightly around her torso. She was staring blankly at the wall behind my uncle so, I reached over and pulled her into my side.

"Well what are they supposed to do now?" my mother said, barely holding back her excitement.

"The FBI has asked us to hold off on doing anything for the time being. He said that they're trying to figure out what's going on, and anything on our end could interfere in the things that they're currently trying to fix. As soon as I'm able, I'll refile," Jimmy murmured. "You should be thankful that I can still practice in Texas."

Her words from earlier felt like an arrow to my soul.

I'll never marry you again.

I could convince her that she didn't really want to be divorced.

Before, I wasn't prepared.

Before, I wasn't as determined.

Before, I hadn't seen my life flash before my eyes, and felt things change inside of me as I was laying on hot asphalt feeling my lifeblood draining out of me.

"Well shit on a stick," my father interjected. "Why couldn't you have just called us? I took a day off of work and everything for this."

I snorted.

My father hated missing work.

Literally despised it.

He'd been working for the same company for well over thirty years, and in all that time, he'd literally taken what added up to a month of time off.

Then again, when you loved your job as much as my father did, I could see why he wouldn't want to leave it.

My father was a youth psychologist and worked with kids day in and day out.

He loved them.

He loved it, even more, when he got to help them work through whatever was bothering them.

He loved seeing them open up and bloom into the person that they would one day become.

"Well," Jimmy rolled his eyes. "I thought this was pretty fucking important. I didn't say you had to come. I said that your boy had to come. He's an adult, though. You don't have to hold his goddamn hand anymore."

My father narrowed his eyes. "The last time you had him in here, you tried to convince him to get a restraining order against your sister."

I grinned.

He had, in fact, done that.

But, to be honest, I'd been fifteen at the time. My mother had decided that she wanted to make sure that I grew up honest and start going to church. I hadn't been to church—unless you counted club meetings for the Dixie Wardens—ever. To a fifteen-year-old boy that had way better things to do than go to church—like drag racing cars because I'd literally found out how awesome that could be the weekend before I'd met with my uncle—the idea of having my free time altered was just unacceptable.

Hence the reason I'd gone to my uncle Jimmy to have him talk reason into his sister.

He'd, of course, been joking when he suggested getting a restraining order. But, the idea had merit at the time.

"Landry…are you okay?" my mother asked.

I looked down and over at the woman that was still in my arms and could see that she was white as a sheet.

"Uh, yeah." She hesitated, then blushed as her eyes caught mine. Likely she was thinking about the comment she'd made before her silent treatment in the truck earlier.

I could just see her thoughts whirling.

If I got my way on this, I might get my way on the other, too.

She narrowed her eyes and looked away, seemingly uninterested.

Except, I could feel the tension in her body as I held her to me.

I also noticed that she didn't once try to get up or do anything to change our positions. She stayed exactly where she was and didn't once try to pull away.

The doorbell over the entryway rang as the door was pushed open, and all talking ceased between us.

My uncle stood and walked over to his next client while the rest of us stayed where we were and tried to process the words that we'd just received.

I wasn't sure it was possible.

Goddamn, I was so excited that I just might burst.

"I guess we could go home," Landry said. "But I'm tired of driving in the truck, to be honest. My hand hurts, and I know your leg has to hurt. Let's get a mot—"

"Absolutely not," my mother disagreed. "We have a pool house, and you'll use it."

I felt my lips quirk.

"Okay," Landry replied, knowing better than to argue with the woman when she was in her current mood.

My mother stood up and clapped her hands excitedly. "Your dad and I will go pick up lunch at the new steakhouse in town. It's amazing, and I think you'll really like it. Medium rare?" she looked at me.

I rolled my eyes. "Is there any other way to eat a steak?"

My dad grunted in agreement.

"I want it…"

"Done," my mother replied with a smile.

"Disgusting," my father replied, a smile on his face, too. "I'm not even sure that restaurant will cook it like that, to be honest. I've heard people laughed out of there a time or two when they ordered something that they didn't want to make."

Landry shrugged. "If that's the case, get me something else. You know what I like."

Landry was a picky eater when it came to meat. Under no circumstances did sushi, fish, or shrimp get anywhere near her.

Though, shrimp didn't get near her at any time because she was allergic to it, though I'd never seen the side effects, and hoped that I never had to.

After hearing that she breaks out in hives and starts swelling with a single bite, I hadn't ever wanted to either.

How About No

Just as I was about to comment, the woman standing in the entryway with her lawyer started to wail, and Jimmy looked at us with a frantic "help me" in his eyes.

Instead of helping him, we chose to leave.

My bladder protested walking past the bathroom, but I'd rather piss myself than talk to a crying woman.

Once I got outside, I immediately took a left down the alley that ran in between my uncle's building and the one next door. The only thing between them was a large dumpster at the end.

"Wade, where are you going?"

"To take a piss."

My mother growled. "Wade Beauregard I will kick your…"

Her voice trailed off the farther I moved down the alley, and by the time I was finished and limping back, my mother was laughing with Landry.

"They have the best chocolate cake," she was saying to my wife.

My wife.

God, it felt so goddamn good to call her that again.

Calling her my ex-wife always felt like I was taking a sharp knife to the heart.

"I'll have that, too." Landry sighed, then turned to me, her cheeks pink. "Are you ready?"

Her words were stiff, and she looked like she was ready to blow.

My lips twitched, and her eyes narrowed, causing me to bite my lip to keep the smile from overtaking my face.

She narrowed her eyes even farther. "Give me your keys, and I'll go get the truck."

Not even thinking about arguing with her after the look in her eyes, I handed over my keys, thankful that I didn't have to make the walk.

First, the drive hadn't been kind, and I was stiff all over. Then, sitting down for that short amount of time only seemed to give me the smallest of reprieves.

Everything hurt—and my leg felt like it was going to fall off any second.

Landry snatched the keys straight from my hand and left without another word, and we all watched her walk off.

Me staring at her ass and thighs in those goddamn shorts that were driving me wild.

My mom in happiness that she was seeing Landry.

My dad? Well, who the hell knew what he was thinking. He was always hard for me to understand motive-wise.

Speaking of…

My father snorted. "Y'all go back to the house. Let the dog out, and we'll go get lunch. This place takes a fuckin' hour to get the shit ready, but their steaks are the best. It'll give you an hour to calm her down."

I snorted.

I'd need it.

"Thanks, Dad."

How About No

Lani Lynn Vale

CHAPTER 9

Pineapple goes on pizza like tongues go into assholes. It's not for everyone, but who are you to judge?

-Text from Wade to Landry

Wade

"My mom wants me to go let her new puppy out," I murmured, trying not to let my eyes linger too long on Landry's shorts. Shorts that were so short that I wouldn't even consider them shorts as much as long underwear. "Do you mind if we go do that first?"

Landry shrugged. "What happened to Boscoe?"

Boscoe had been my mother's Jack Russel Terrier who had been older than dirt. He'd died last year of a heart attack while my parents had been asleep.

"Dead," I said simply.

Her breath inhaled deeply. "Your mom loved him."

She had.

"She did," I confirmed. "And she's still trying to get over it, to be honest. Dad brought her this dog to hopefully help her get out of her funk. He'd have brought her one earlier if she could've decided what breed she wanted. Eventually, we decided to find her a rescue."

I saw Landry melt a little bit.

"I almost got one from your rescue," I admitted. "But I didn't want her to get attached to another dog and have that one die on her, too. I felt it was kind of the wrong thing to do in that situation."

She smiled at me sadly. "Not all of the ones I'm getting lately are old, though. Some of them are just so broken and or unwanted that they have nowhere else to go. Sure, the majority of the ones that I'm getting are older, but we're branching out into some battered souls with missing body parts."

I grinned as I pushed open the door. "Watch out, he's rather feisty."

I hadn't actually seen him in a while, but what I remembered of him had me bracing my legs and hoping that the dog wouldn't barrel into me like a freight train like he had the last time.

Luckily, Rover didn't come barreling out.

He came at us quietly and softly, almost as if he'd realized that we were both hurt.

"Awww," Landry said as she dropped down to her knees.

I stopped her before she could make it all the way down.

"Pet him outside. Mom says he pees when he's excited," I ordered. "I don't want to be cleaning up pee."

She snorted but did as I asked, walking farther into the house and closing the door.

Instead of stopping to pet the puppy, who was looking at us and wagging his tail, we both shuffled past him to the back door and walked outside.

Rover followed us outside, did his business, and immediately came to Landry who was once again crouched on the ground waiting for him.

"Is he a pure bloodhound?" she asked.

I shrugged and walked to the swing and took a seat, groaning audibly when the pressure on my leg finally diminished.

"I don't think so," I admitted. "He might be, but we don't really know."

She hummed and petted the dog's ears for a few long minutes before the dog finally broke away from her and started to explore.

"Mom says that if he finds a scent, he's occupied for hours." He paused. "Which is why he was at the shelter to begin with. He wanders. Doesn't do cages well. Dad said that they let him out sometimes in the morning, and he doesn't come back until the sun is going down."

"Coonhounds are notorious for that," she murmured. "They're easily distracted by scents and will follow it all the way back to its source if they're interested enough."

"Guess we're just lucky that they live off in the middle of a hundred acres," I admitted, shifting slightly on the seat when I saw she was looking to sit down, too.

Once there was enough room, she took her seat next to me and started to gently push the swing with her toes.

And although it was causing me pain, I let her do it because I knew that she loved to rock.

We sat in silence like that for about five minutes before she said, "This is bad."

And suddenly I got angry.

So. Fucking. Angry.

"It's not bad," I snapped. "It's the best thing that's ever happened."

It gives me a fighting chance to show her that I was no longer the dumb, useless piece of shit that I was to her when I found out about her sister.

I just needed time!

She looked at me like I'd lost my mind. "You don't think that being back together is going to blow up in our faces?"

I tried to remain calm, even though the idea that she didn't want to be with me still stung. "How would it?"

She crossed her arms over her chest and said, "Oh, I don't know. You've turned your whole club against me. Everyone in town looks at me like I'm a pariah, and I'm living with another man! Let's not forget about that date I saw you on a few days ago."

I frowned. "I haven't been on a date. I haven't *wanted* to be on a date. I don't fucking want anybody but you."

Please give me a chance.

She frowned. "I saw you. You were eating at a diner with a woman."

"I was eating at a diner with a woman because I was almost done, there were no other tables, and I invited her to sit with me while I took the last bite of my hamburger," I countered. "Which you would've known had you had the balls to actually talk to me when you came in instead of glaring holes through me."

She opened her mouth, then closed it, seemingly stunned speechless.

"And my club doesn't hate you. They're worried about me, and they know that I still love you." I paused. "Which is not a bad thing. As for another man? I think it's time that we stop beating around the bush. You haven't been with anyone else and likely never would. Please. Give us a chance."

Her mouth dropped open. "I know that, but your club thinks I am. I get no respect from them. Your friends would cross the street to avoid walking past me."

There was no denying it. They had my best interests at heart.

She got a worried look on her face, and when she started to stand up, I had no other option but to pull her into my arms and deposit her sideways on my lap to keep her from leaving.

The moment that her fine ass made contact with my lap, she started to squirm and pull away.

I refused to let her.

Locking my arms around her, I held tight, despite that her movements were making my leg jostle causing shards of pain to shoot along the nerve endings in my leg.

"Let me go!" she ordered fiercely.

I laughed.

In her face.

She narrowed her eyes and reached for me with her hands. Both buried in my hair as she tried to use leverage to push herself away.

Different shards of pain shot through me, but this pain was most welcome.

I wanted her hands in my hair.

I loved her hands in my hair.

I loved her hands on my body.

I smiled, and she got even more angry.

"Never. I'm never letting you go. All I need is time. Time to convince you that I won't ever put anyone else first. Only you."

***

Landry

Things had gone from bad to worse.

As if hearing that we were still married hadn't been enough, Wade then took me to his parents' home and proceeded to tell me that he wanted to stay married. That all he needed was time to convince me.

Was he crazy?

Yes, yes he was.

The fact that I was happy about the fact that I was still married to him should've been frightening. But it wasn't. It wasn't scary at all. It felt right.

Which *was* what scared me.

And when I'd tried to leave, Wade had grabbed me and pulled me into his lap—locking those strong arms around me and refusing to let me go.

I'd squirmed, pushed, and struggled all to no avail.

He wasn't letting me get away.

I'd buried my hands in his hair, trying to force myself away from him and cause him enough pain to let me go—but he'd held strong.

"Let me go now, or I'll hurt you, and I really don't want to hurt you," I hissed, letting one hand go to move to his bicep. There, I dug my nails in and started to rake them up and down his arms.

He didn't flinch.

In fact, he grinned wider.

"Gonna take more than your claws to hurt me, baby," he informed me, his eyes alight with mischief.

He was enjoying this, even though I could see that I was causing him at least some pain in his injured leg.

He was enjoying this immensely.

I wanted to claw his eyes out and wipe that smug, satisfied, superior look off his stupid, pretty face.

I struggled harder, being careful not to hurt my hand which I could feel starting to throb from all the movement, as well as keep most of my weight off of his injured leg.

And if I was hurting, my struggling was likely hurting him, too.

Yet he wasn't saying a word.

He kept his mouth shut and put up with my struggles.

"God," I hissed, giving one final attempt.

I squirmed out of the seated position he had me in and got my knees up and ended up practically straddling his body facing him.

All I ended up accomplishing was wedging the solid column of muscle and flesh that I'd been studiously ignoring with everything that I had further between my thighs. Now, it was pressed perfectly between the gap in my ass cheeks and I was frozen solid.

I leaned forward and put my face into his, all the while whispering words that I didn't mean—and never had.

"I don't want to do this," I hissed.

He laughed in my face again, causing me to recoil.

I narrowed my eyes and leaned forward to tell him off, but he responded before I could. "That's your problem, hellcat. You don't want me this close to you because you don't trust yourself. You love me. You've loved me from the moment that you saw me just like I've loved you from the moment I first saw you. I knew you were the one the moment you walked through that classroom door. I knew the moment that you walked away from me that I couldn't wait to see you again. I just knew. Because my soul recognized its soulmate. And you're it. You're the other half of my soul, and I can't find a single thing wrong with being back where we were always meant to be."

"You don't see a problem?" I shrieked. "We're married again! You chose someone else over me! Someone who's *always* been chosen over me!"

He sobered instantly. "And you will never understand how sorry I am that I didn't put you first. That I didn't see what I was doing when I did it. If I had…if I had, I would've been able to prevent spending all these months in a perpetual state of torture because you weren't there by my side."

I clenched my teeth and bared them at him.

God, his face. His sexy bearded chin drove me wild. I just wanted to plant my fist into it.

He wouldn't be hurt by it, though.

He'd love it.

He'd love anything as long as it came from me.

Which stopped me in my tracks.

All the venom and rancor, all the uneasiness and need to get away—it just vanished.

I stilled and loosened up on my hands, allowing them both to drop to my lap.

He didn't let up a single bit as he waited for what I'd do next.

"Nothing I say will matter, will it?" I asked, feeling something inside of my chest tighten.

He shook his head.

His perfect hair shifted, causing a lock of it to fall over those green eyes that I loved so much.

"No, baby," he answered honestly. "Because I was always going to fight for you. I was always going to make sure that you had what you wanted. What you needed. And baby, what you need is me."

I looked away and studied the rolling hills that blanketed Porter and Minnie's massive backyard.

"You let me leave," I whispered brokenly.

He dropped his forehead onto my shoulder. "I was so hurt when I got the papers from that nurse. You never even gave me a chance. I wanted to fight for you, but you wouldn't give me a chance. I also knew that if I didn't let you go, you'd find a way to do it without my help. You were that determined. But honey, I was also determined. I knew that one day I'd be back…I was biding my time. Each day, I made sure I found a way for you to see me. For you to realize what you were missing…and it worked, didn't it?"

It had.

I thought back to how he seemed to show up wherever I was, no matter how hard I tried to avoid him. Whether it be him dropping his uniform shirt off for me to sew a button on it while I was at work, to arriving at my dog rescue to help me unload the pallet of dog food just to turn around and leave once it was accomplished. And nary a word was ever said between us. He was just there, and I was just letting him be there. It didn't matter that I never said a word. He wouldn't allow that to deter him.

Little things like him pulling up to get gas while I was at the gas station and pumping it for me, to him making sure to send me flowers even though he never signed them.

He really hadn't left me, had he? I didn't go out of my way to see him, but he always ended up in my vicinity.

He'd made sure that he was always on my mind.

I inhaled a shaky breath, then blew it out.

Moments after that…my mouth found his.

And that was all she wrote.

I was done.

The moment my lips touched his—the moment my tongue tangled with his—I knew that what we had would be forever. That, even if we weren't together, he was always going to be mine.

Because he was right.

He was my soulmate.

And I was fighting a losing battle.

He groaned into my mouth, and one of his hands loosened from around my waist to run up the length of my spine to bury itself in my hair.

I shivered when he gently slanted my head to get a better angle…and then I was reminded why Wade had always done it for me.

I had absolutely zero control when it came to the man.

All he had to do was get near me, and I turned into this passionately obsessed woman that lived and breathed Wade Johnson.

"Dear sweet baby Jesus," I breathed when he finally pulled back. "This is the worst idea ever."

He didn't answer me.

Instead, he pulled me to him once again, and I decided that maybe I was tired of fighting everything.

I was tired of fighting me. I was tired of fighting us. I was just plain tired.

I needed Wade, and I needed him now.

Everything else? The marriage. The way I'd felt betrayed. The promises I'd made to myself.

That was all background music.

Being in Wade's arms was where I had always wanted to be.

I moaned and leaned forward into the kiss, my uninjured hand clenching his hair while my injured one went to cup his neck.

His pulse was beating a fast, hard *thump-thump* against my palm, and I pulled back so that he could see me.

"This really shouldn't happen here," I admitted.

He snorted and reached for my shirt.

We both knew it was going to happen exactly where we were.

I just hoped his parents didn't come home while we were doing it.

"Since when have we ever done it anywhere appropriate?" he inquired.

That was true.

Our first time we'd done it on the front seat of his truck in the middle of town. Our second time we'd at least parked his bike in a secluded spot in my apartment complex's parking lot before we'd gotten busy.

The third had been on a park bench and our fourth had been in a swing much like the one we were on—only in his backyard.

Hell, we hadn't even made it to the privacy of his bedroom until well after our four-month mark.

When we saw each other—which was rare since he was always busy with work, and I was busy with school and work—we barely had enough time to wait until we were somewhere where we wouldn't be seen.

And it looked like time and distance didn't change how we went about doing certain things—like sex.

We were all about spontaneity.

"Arms up," he whispered against my lips.

I pulled back and allowed him to pull them up, shivering when his eyes found my breasts.

"You're wearing my bra," he growled.

I was.

I liked wearing what he considered 'his bra.'

It was a black lace see-through number that he'd bought me to wear on our honeymoon.

But it never stayed on long when he was around and knew I was wearing it.

Honestly, today was literally the longest I'd ever worn it when he was in the vicinity.

If it wasn't so freakin' sad, it actually would've been kind of funny.

"God, you destroy me," he murmured, pulling his arm from around me and trailing his finger down the curve of my left breast.

I swallowed hard and squirmed, causing him to growl.

"And those godforsaken shorts," he hissed. "Where the fuck did you find those at?"

I smiled. "Sam's. They're considered 'CrossFit' shorts. But I thought they were cute, so I bought them. This is my first time wearing them."

He growled low in his throat. "So, you decided to wear them when you knew that I wouldn't be able to touch you."

I tilted my head slightly. "As you can see, you're touching me right now."

In fact, one of his hands was cupping my breast, while the other was spanning the curve of my ass. The hand on my ass had fingers that were getting perilously close to other more intimate parts of my anatomy with each passing second.

"Touching you," he agreed. "I guess I should show you what 'touching' really is."

Then he reached around me even farther and grabbed the inside hem of my shorts and yanked them over, exposing my inner flesh.

I gasped when I felt the cool air where I really shouldn't feel cool air while still mostly wearing shorts and said, "God."

He leaned forward and sucked the cord of my neck while his talented fingers dragged slowly through my folds.

My very wet, embarrassingly slick folds.

"All for me," he declared.

I shifted again, dragging my clit over the rough crotch of his jeans, knowing without a shadow of a doubt that I'd just likely stained his pants with my juices.

Neither one of us gave a shit.

For me, it was because feeling that denim against my sensitive nerve endings shot a jolt of pleasure through me, and for him, the pressure of that movement just made him want more.

How did I know he wanted more?

Because he pulled the shorts and panties down my legs, putting me right back where I was, then dropped both of his hands to my hips and ground himself up, pressing us tightly together so that this time when he repeated what I'd just done, even more sensation poured through us.

I bent my head down and buried it in his neck, my teeth latching on to the muscle right at the base of his neck.

When he did it again, I bit down even harder—not hard enough to draw blood, but there would definitely be some marks when we were through.

Wade had always liked sex wild and rough.

Me? I didn't necessarily know what I did or didn't like back then until Wade taught me everything I'd ever need to know. I'd been a virgin when I met him. A big flippin' virgin that had absolutely no clue whatsoever what she was getting into when she agreed to take a man like Wade into her bed.

What I hadn't known at the time was that Wade was just as inexperienced as me, though he in no way, shape or form acted like it.

But, over the course of our courtship and marriage, Wade had taught me a lot of things, and those things were things that I greatly missed while we'd been separated since our supposed divorce.

I hadn't realized just how addicted I'd become to the man until I'd walked away from him.

"Unbutton my pants," he urged.

I didn't waste time reaching in between us.

I didn't stop at the twinge of pain that ran through my hand and up my arm when I roughly yanked his jeans open. I didn't stop until his jeans were gaping and his dick was in the palm of my hand.

And suddenly, everything was right in my world.

I had him back.

I had him in my hand.

I had him exactly where I wanted him.

Our life was still fucked up and everything was still up in the air, but right then? We were exactly where we were meant to be.

And then he urged me up on my knees and pushed until his cock was lodged at my entrance.

My eyes caught his when he started to slowly force me down, taking everything that he had to give. I felt our souls reconnect right then, back to how we were in the very beginning.

Sex had never been our problem.

It'd always been so fucking good for us.

And this, him filling me up one slow inch at a time? It reminded me exactly why I hadn't been able to move on.

There was no moving on from Wade Beauregard Johnson. There was only existing until you died.

My breath caught when he finally hit bottom, and just when I thought he wouldn't get any more in, that there was literally no more of me for him to fill, he pulled out and started the whole entire thing all over again.

And, just sayin', the man made me take more.

I felt so full. So, fucking full that I felt like I might burst from the inside out.

His eyes were locked on mine, and he was reading my slight panic.

"You're tight," he rasped, barely able to control his breathing. "So fucking tight."

I wanted to laugh.

I hadn't had anything inside of me but a finger since him. Of course, I was tight! His dick was bigger than anything I'd ever had inside of me in my life. Hell, he'd come around and given me the best that any woman could have, and I had no reason for dildos and vibrators. The moment that he came into my life I'd thrown them all away. Even when we'd separated, I hadn't bought any more.

What would be the point when you knew there was something so much better out there than you were capable of getting?

As Wade started to move me up and down, my eyes drifted closed, and I remembered exactly why he was so much better.

He filled me so completely—so utterly full—that at times I was sure that I would find it hard to walk after we were through. But during the actual act of sex? I could care less what I'd feel like afterward because Wade could do things to my body that I never even dreamed of.

Like when he pushed me back slightly, causing my hands to either go to his knees that were steady behind me, or fall backward.

I deposited both of my hands right on his shoulders and squeezed, changing the angle he was entering me, and I saw stars.

That was my spot.

For some reason, when I was on top and in this exact same position, things always went quickly.

I knew just as well as he knew that he hadn't had anybody since me. Meaning he was likely just as close if not closer than I was.

He always used to say that being inside of me was like being inside a hot, wet silken fist that hugged him like a leather glove made for him.

I had always agreed, because when he was inside of me, I felt like if he were any bigger, I just might burst at the seams.

"Fuck me," he growled, his face a mixture of pain and pleasure.

It was then I realized that all the rocking and jerking of my hips and thighs were likely forcing him to move when he was hurt.

But when I went to move off, he stopped me with a forceful touch of his hand on my breast, urging me to keep moving on top of him. "No, don't."

How About No

I didn't stop.

I was so freakin' close that I *couldn't* stop.

"Goddamn, faster," he urged, helping me move.

The swing we were in was shimmying and shaking, swaying almost violently with our movements.

My knees hurt where they were digging into the wooden slats, and I was fairly sure I had a splinter somewhere on my shin.

But, as he continued to pump into me, I no longer cared.

I cried out as a tidal wave of pleasure slammed into me.

My pussy clenched around him as I started to come.

Things got very wet very quickly, and I had a second to realize that I shouldn't be that wet when another orgasm slammed into me.

I'd never, not ever, been a multiple-orgasm person.

But as he fucked me hard and followed me over the edge, I wasn't sure that I wouldn't continue to be.

The man was good—and I'd missed him.

God, how I'd missed him.

I leaned forward until my body was pressed against his chest, and felt his cock continue to jerk inside of me.

I also made sure to shift my weight to the side so that as little of my weight as possible was on his bad side.

Soon the only thing that was moving was the swing as he swayed lazily, and I wondered then and there what the hell I was going to do now.

"Are you okay?" I asked softly.

I felt him swallow against my forehead. "Leg hurts like a bitch now that I'm not focused on coming," he admitted. "But goddamn, did I need that."

I laughed and started to move, ignoring the way that my knees ached and my shin stung.

It was only when I was standing that I realized he was really wet.

"Uhhhh," I looked at him, horrified.

He grinned. "Didn't know that you were such a juicy comer before, but now that I know…we'll have to continue to play with that."

I felt my face flush as he stood. "Now let's go see if we can get cleaned up before my parents get back with our steaks and wonder why we're flushed and panting."

CHAPTER 10

You know what's worse than the first day of school? Being out of school and realizing that you have to work and pay bills and shit.

-Landry to Wade

Landry

That night, I slept in Wade's bed.

After staying up late, talking and drinking with his parents, and genuinely having one of the best nights of my life, I wasn't going to say no to sleeping with him again.

Honestly, the word "no" hadn't even crossed my mind as we mutually got ready for bed.

And now, in the light of morning, I was wondering what in the hell I was going to do when we got home.

Regardless of whether or not we really were still married, we still had a lot to work out. We were still exactly where we were before we'd found out that we were still tied irrevocably together.

But, the thought of doing anything—signing divorce papers all over again—was abhorrent to me.

It'd literally taken me getting drunk the night before the bone marrow extraction surgery—I was also semi-hoping that if I had an alcohol content in my blood, they'd refuse to do surgery, which, by the way, didn't stop them at all—to get those papers signed.

I honestly didn't think that I could sign them again.

I'd felt raw and broken for months after I'd signed them—after he'd signed them—and if I was being honest, still did.

Something had lifted off my chest yesterday when I'd heard his uncle's words.

The control that I'd thought I wielded was taken from me, and I'd never felt more alive.

Then again, it could be the hot hunk of a man sleeping next to me.

I rolled slightly so that I was facing him and stared at the man that made my heart pound just by being near him.

He was still very much asleep. How could I tell? He was snoring through his slightly open mouth.

His breaths were steady and even, and he'd likely stay that way for the next hour or two seeing as it was still ungodly early. I woke up like clockwork at four-thirty in the morning due to having to be at the daycare at six to open it.

I was honestly surprised that my phone hadn't started to ring. It was unusual for things to actually go the way they were supposed to with my employees.

I just hoped the reason I hadn't gotten a phone call yet was because everything was running smoothly and not because they were all on their death beds and unable to get to work.

Feeling the protest of my bladder reminds me that it wasn't happy with me and all the beer I'd had the night before, I pushed carefully from the bed and headed to the bathroom.

I only turned the light on once I had the door quietly closed.

When my eyes finally adjusted, I did my business and went to the sink to wash my hands, only to be stopped by the multiple pill bottles that lined the edge of the sink.

I scanned each bottle, studying the labels, and felt my heart start to pound again.

That day that he was hurt was the scariest day of my life, and that wasn't because I'd been shot myself. It was because my worst nightmare had come true, and Wade had been shot in the line of duty.

He was alive now, but there was never a promise or guarantee when it came to a police officer's life. There was always the possibility that he'd strap that Kevlar vest on himself, and have a paramedic slice it off of him as they worked tirelessly over his battered body.

I shivered and pushed the bottles farther to the side, making sure not to get them wet as I washed my hands and face, followed shortly by brushing my teeth with the toothbrush I hadn't been aware of getting out on my own last night.

Fresh and clean once again, I turned off the light and walked back out into the main room of the pool house.

With the eerie blue glow coming in through the glass windows of the room, I could make out Wade's sleeping form in the bed.

He'd changed positions while I'd been gone. Now he was on his back, his good leg cocked up and leaning to the side. His arms were up over his chest, fingers crossed, and he was snoring softly once again, only this time his mouth was wide open.

I felt a smile reach my face, and I contemplated getting back into bed with him.

But something he'd said last night as we were walking inside—about how he hadn't been sleeping all that well since he'd been shot—forced me not to.

I wanted him to get all the sleep he could get.

Not only was it better to help him in general, but it would help him heal faster—or so I'd heard.

Tiptoeing to the door, I opened it and disappeared outside, closing it just as quietly behind me.

I was unsurprised to see Porter sitting outside drinking a cup of coffee. He was sitting in a lawn chair with the morning newspaper in his hands, reading by the light that the kitchen LED lights cast through the glass.

He looked up from his paper when he heard me approach, and grinned.

"Thought for sure you'd sleep until noon since you only went to bed about four hours ago," he murmured as I walked up and took the seat beside him.

I snorted. "It doesn't matter what I do. I'm always up by four-thirty. I guess I have an internal alarm. I have to be to the daycare by six, and if I don't get up early, then I won't have time to get any housework done. Sometimes I catch a bug and workout, but those times are few and far between. Mostly I sit there like you're doing, read the newspaper and drink coffee until I feel human enough to do something."

He grunted. "Sounds about right. Go get you some coffee. Read the funnies."

He slapped the 'funnies' down in front of me and I stood back up to do his bidding, happy to feel that my hand was doing much better today than it had yesterday. I barely had a throb when I put pressure against it now—though my hand had been numb since I'd woken up.

Coffee in hand, I retook my seat and started scanning over the comics.

We sat like that in companionable silence for what felt like forever but ended up being more like thirty minutes.

As he finished with a section of his paper, he'd lay it down in a stack next to my elbow, and I'd pick it up once I was finished with the one he'd previously handed me.

It continued like that until he finally set the last section down and waited for me to finish.

Since it wasn't my town, I skimmed a few of the articles, but ultimately put it down a whole lot faster than I would have if we were home. I did stop to scan the "ask the editor" section, smiling when I saw a letter about how there needed to be more news articles and fewer articles about unimportant "shit" that nobody cared about.

"Why does that letter sound like something one of your boys would write?" I teased.

One of his "boys" referenced the men in his motorcycle club, The Dixie Wardens.

My eyes lifted to find Porter staring at me, studying my face.

"Probably because it was," he laughed. "Dixie's tired of reading about fake news. He wants the cold hard facts, and the paper is trying to cater—like it should—to both political parties."

I hummed in assent as I folded the paper back the way it'd been and laid it in the finished stack.

"You had a lot to say last night," he murmured. "Do you still feel like that in the light of day?"

I felt my heart start to pound. "Feel like what?"

He grinned slightly. "Do you remember talking to me while Wade and Minnie got the coffee and cookies last night?"

I did. Bits and pieces anyway.

"Some," I admitted.

"You remember mentioning that you were scared?"

I blinked. "No."

"You said you were scared of what life was going to bring now that you were once again married to Wade," he reminded me. "You also said that his job scared the crap out of you. That you wanted his babies and couldn't give them to him, and also that you were fairly sure that once he knew the real you, he'd leave."

I pressed the heels of my hands to my face as I groaned. "I'm not sure any of that was true."

Lies. All lies.

"Sometimes the things people say when they're drunk, and their brain isn't able to control their filter, are the truest things that have ever been said," he explained. "And I do think you're scared. You have a right to be scared. But I also think that it was the dumbest thing in the world for Wade to allow you to leave and not fight the divorce."

I dropped my hands and stared at him. "Wade let me go because he was forced to."

He snorted in derision. "That's the biggest load of crap ever. He wanted you more than he wanted his next breath. He feels for you like I feel for Minnie. And let me tell you something. I once gave Minnie up because I thought it'd be better for her to be sad than to be married to a fella like me who would only bring her down. But then we were both miserable as hell. What is the point of staying apart when you're happier together?"

I pressed my lips tightly shut.

"Don't think I don't know that you still love him," Porter said. "Y'all have tried the being apart thing—and for what? You are both miserable. Y'all both still love each other. The things that you fought over are in the past. You need him just like he needs you. He may need you more now than he ever needed you before, though."

His leg.

He was talking about the possibility of Wade losing his leg.

"He's never needed me, Porter," I explained softly. "It was always me doing the leaning, not the other way around."

"And that, girl, is where you're wrong." He stood up and grabbed for his coffee cup. "My boy's needed you since the moment that you came on to his radar, and you just didn't know it."

With that, he walked inside, leaving me alone to my own thoughts.

I shivered as a particularly sharp breeze rolled over the open field that Porter and Minnie built their house on.

Standing myself, I walked back inside the pool house and closed the door—a little too hard.

Wade lifted his sleepy face from the pillow the moment I shut it, and he frowned. "You okay?"

No, I wasn't okay.

I walked over to the bed and stared at Wade's sleep-creased face and wondered if I was making the worst mistake of my life.

"Landry?"

I put a knee on the bed, then leaned over his big body, staring at him long and hard until I finally came to a decision.

"When we get home, I need you to give me a couple of days to think," I said softly.

His eyebrows lowered as if he wasn't happy with that possibility.

"And right now?" he growled.

"It's impossible to think with you around," I told him honestly.

He chuckled softly.

Then I gasped when he grabbed me by the hips and pulled me down roughly.

"Then right now you won't mind if I do this?"

No. I didn't mind. I didn't mind at all.

My mouth opened, and I marveled in the fact that he was able to find what he was aiming for without consciously trying.

"How'd you know I didn't have panties on?" I asked roughly.

He'd filled me in one thrust.

Everything inside of me was tight in anticipation.

My pussy was filled to bursting, things stretched that should've been loosened beforehand, and honestly, it felt like being on the verge of pain.

Yet...I wanted it.

I needed it.

He skimmed his hands up the t-shirt, stopping when he found my breasts.

I sat up and let him play with my nipples, sitting still on his cock.

Likely he was trying to give me time to adjust, and normally I'd be thankful.

This time, I wanted it to hurt.

"Wade, I need..." I rasped.

And suddenly I found myself on my back with Wade's big body hovering over mine.

My hands went to his shoulder blades as he roughly yanked my legs up, practically shoving them to my chest.

Then he was powering into me, taking me so hard and fast that I couldn't think.

"God, baby," he growled, his mouth slanting over mine to take me with a rough, soul-searing kiss. "You take my breath away."

I refrained from saying my usual "that's because you're doing some high-quality cardio" quick-witted reply when he used to take me this hard and fast. But my brain was being scrambled, and I couldn't open my mouth to breathe, let alone supply a coherent response.

My neck stretched as I ground my head into the bed.

The pillows around my face were suffocating me, but I was willing to trade a little brain damage for the orgasm that I could feel was about to overtake me.

The only thing that could be heard in the room was our heavy breathing and the slap-slap of his pelvis connecting with mine.

His balls were also slapping against my asshole with each rough thrust, and it was rendering me unable to think.

Hell, everything about the man had always done that.

His smile.

His penis.

His hands.

Everything about him was freaking perfect.

I was so lost in chasing after my orgasm that I didn't anticipate the bite to my breast until he was already sinking those teeth of his into my skin.

The sharp pain was apparently what I needed because the next second I was coming so hard that the house could've caught fire around us and I wouldn't have cared.

My pussy pulsed and squeezed, causing him to curse harshly against my breast.

My fingernails dug into his shoulders.

My legs tightened around him to the point where I was sure I'd have bruises from where his hip bones dug into me.

And then there was the way his cock started to jerk inside of me, filling me with so much cum that I could feel it leaking out the sides.

Then he stilled, and I flopped my limbs uselessly to the bed as I laid there and tried to catch my breath.

He moved the pillows from my face, allowing me to have blessed fresh air, and grinned down at me.

I swallowed hard, loving that face more than I loved anything in the world.

"I'll give you two days," he growled. "Nothing more…now go into the bathroom and get me a pain pill. I think my leg is about to fall off."

CHAPTER 11

Sorry I'm late, I got here as soon as I wanted to.

-Coffee Cup

Landry

I looked down at the retired military working dog and wondered if there was anything that I could do that hadn't already been tried with him.

He'd come to me as a last resort, and I honestly hated that for him.

He looked so sweet with his graying face and his soulful brown eyes.

But then you tried to get close to him, and things went south.

Like right now, I was staring at his paws, wondering if I could get close to him, and realized rather quickly after scooting nearer that it wasn't going to happen.

This situation needed a man's touch.

I needed my husband.

My not-so-ex-husband had been relegated to desk duty today after his doctor appointment where he'd obviously got news he did not enjoy hearing. I'd found this out from Bayou, who again met me for lunch on our park bench because it was going on day three and he'd not once contacted me like I'd expected him to.

I looked down at my almost-healed hand and wondered if what I was about to do was the best decision and realized that it probably was the stupidest one I could make.

But, unable to stop myself, I rolled the dog's cage back up into my van and situated it. Once I had it nicely tucked in, I firmly swung the van's door closed and then circled around the van.

Once I was inside, I started the van up and took one more glance over my shoulder at the dog in the cage.

He snarled at me.

I shivered and started the van.

I would not give up on this dog, just like I would not give up on my husband.

There were a lot of things that I'd realized over the last seventy-two hours, and all of them centered around the fact that I only had one life.

I needed to live it to the best of my ability.

And that included taking him up on his offer and trying to make something of our relationship.

Starting the van, I merged onto the road and gasped when a black motorcycle darted out in front of me, causing me to nearly hit it.

"Shit!" I gasped.

I hadn't seen it at all.

"I'm so sorry!" I yelled at the man.

The man pulled over and got off the bike so fast that my heart started to palpitate.

He stalked toward my van, and I looked into the man's angry eyes and wondered what he was going to do.

My hands clenched on the steering wheel, and I started to shake as the biker stopped in front of the hood of my van.

He slammed his hand down hard on the hood, and I jumped.

His angry gray eyes met mine, and I bit my lip. "I'm sorry," I said to him again.

He flipped me off and walked away.

Dropping my head to my steering wheel, I counted to ten.

At number five, the motorcycle roared off.

At number seven, someone honked behind me.

I opened my eyes at number ten, looked around—this time much more thoroughly—and started out once again. But as I drove, I became angry.

I'd looked for him.

Hell, it was nearly impossible not to see motorcyclists since my husband was one of them. I counted them. I instinctively listened for them. It was unthinkable for me to do what I'd just done today, and the only reason that I could find that I hadn't seen that particular one was that he was going extremely fast in a residential neighborhood.

I might've tuned out the roar of his engine but when something comes up on you that freakin' fast, it's almost impossible to prepare.

I'd worked myself into a bad mood by the time I pulled up to Wade's place.

It was a small two-bedroom duplex in the middle of town, and I'd hated it the moment he got it because of the girl he shared the other half of the duplex with.

And, to make matters worse, the girl that used the other half of the duplex was outside talking to my man—and the man that I'd nearly smashed with my van—as I pulled up.

Son of a bitch.

I contemplated leaving but chose not to, instead trying to ignore them all while I went to the cage at the back of the van.

Ignoring the discussion going on in the front yard, I opened the van's door and felt my heart skip a few beats at the snarls coming from the cage.

The dog was snarling and snapping at the cage now, and I just…lost it.

Sitting down, my ass on the curb, I dropped my head into my hands and started to cry.

Crying was actually not a good word for it. Sobbing was more to my liking.

After three days of not coming up with anything other than I missed my husband, and then having to deal with the dog that seriously hated me, I couldn't help it.

The dog's situation was dismal.

He was seven years old, and in addition to the German Shepherd's age, he'd been a military working dog that had retired from service. The reason he'd retired was due to an attack that had left him maimed—and without a back leg.

To make matters worse, his handler—as well as the handler's entire unit—had died in the same explosion, and there was nobody that was willing to work with the dog.

He'd been scheduled for euthanasia in freakin' Oklahoma due to the inability to work with the severely traumatized dog when I'd heard about him through my Facebook page. I'd gone to get him this morning

There was another group that was trying to adopt him so they could help him, but the dog wasn't responding well to their handling. I was more qualified and hoped that I would be able to break through to this dedicated service dog.

He was in bad shape.

Due to nobody being able to get close to him, the dog had suffered. He'd been in a cage since he'd woken up legless, he was volatile and snapped at anyone who got close enough and was honestly beyond even my reach.

But I just couldn't stand for him to be put to sleep without at least trying.

Which led me to now.

Sitting on my ass.

With the dog snapping and snarling at the cage, and my ex-husband talking to two people that I'd rather not talk to right then.

I heard someone's shoe scuff the surface of the concrete right behind me, and suddenly I was up and in Wade's arms.

I buried my face into his neck and sobbed.

I sobbed because of the dog.

I sobbed because of the news that I'd heard from Bayou about Wade's leg.

I sobbed because I'd almost killed someone without meaning to.

I sobbed because I'd been wrong.

I should've never left Wade.

I'd ruined our lives all because I was too stupid to realize that Wade wouldn't have been upset with me over refusing to donate bone marrow to my sister. He would've been disappointed, but he wouldn't have hated me like I'd thought he would.

And the fight we'd had the morning of my sister's impending doom about children could've been avoided too had I just opened up and spoken with him.

My breath hitched, and Wade ran his hand up my back soothingly, staying bent at an awkward angle as I practically hung off of his neck. He had to be uncomfortable, but not once did he shift his body or complain. He stayed holding me tightly.

Eventually my sobbing lessened, and I loosened my hold on his neck.

When I did, he stood up straighter but didn't let me go.

I opened my eyes from where I'd had my face buried in his neck and turned my head, blinking at the steel gray eyes of the man that'd slammed his hand down on the hood of my van earlier.

He didn't look pissed anymore.

In fact, he looked…tortured.

"You okay, honey?" Wade asked, pushing me away slightly so that he could see my face.

I gave him what he wanted and looked up into his eyes, smiling sadly at him. "I'm sorry. It's just…I've had a really bad day."

The dog's snarls hadn't abated, and in fact, had ramped up to terrifying as more people had come closer to his cage.

"What's this one's story?" Wade asked, dropping a kiss on my mouth.

I returned the kiss for the few seconds that he gave me to enjoy it, and then turned in his arms to stare at the snarling dog.

The man at our side came closer, his eyes taking in the dog right along with us.

I looked over at him. "I'm sorry for nearly killing you."

He looked at me and grinned. "I didn't realize you had a dog in the back of your van making this kind of racket, or I would've understood."

I swallowed hard.

"Baby, this is Hoax. He's the one we told you about that's Delta. He's here for a few weeks on leave in between missions," Wade explained. "And you almost killed him?"

"I was distracted," I admitted, gesturing toward the dog. "And I pulled out without clearly checking my mirrors, though, just sayin', you were driving really fast in a residential neighborhood. You probably should stop doing that."

Hoax snorted. "Yeah, my cousin sent me a text saying the same damn thing as I was leaving today."

This Hoax character was nice…now.

Then, when I'd almost killed him with my vehicle, he'd been a hell of a lot scarier.

He looked a lot like Wade—at least in build. But he had pale skin and gray eyes compared to Wade's lightly sun-bronzed skin and green eyes. Hoax also had a really bushy beard whereas Wade's was trimmed due to the regulations he had to abide by to be a Bear Bottom Police Officer.

Honestly, the more I looked at Hoax, the more freaked out I got.

He was a seriously scary individual—even if he wasn't pissed off anymore that I'd nearly killed him.

"Anyway, I'm sorry I was such a shit," he said apologetically. "I was in a recent motorcycle wreck and it's put me in a perpetually bad mood."

He held up the arm that was farthest away from me, and it was then that I saw he had a black cast underneath his leather jacket.

"Wow," I said. "I'm sorry. That makes me feel even worse."

Wade let me go to move toward the cage, and suddenly, the dog's snarling just…stopped.

I gasped.

"I'm sorry to be a bother," I heard from behind me. "But do you mind moving the van so that it's not blocking my half of the driveway?"

I stiffened.

"It's not blocking your driveway," Hoax grunted. "It's obstructing half of Wade's half of the driveway."

I swallowed hard, unsure what to say to the woman.

In all technicality, she was right. My van was blocking half of the driveway, but only because all the other parking spots were taken by various trucks, cars, and motorcycles. There was literally nowhere else to park except for the driveway itself—which I wasn't going to do seeing as it wasn't my home.

"True," the woman agreed. "But technically we share the driveway, and with you parked in my half of the driveway, I need to be able to utilize his half of the driveway."

Hoax growled and turned on his heels, stalking toward his bike.

Seconds later, he was rolling it backward onto Wade's half of the driveway and then leaning it back to rest on the kickstand once again.

"Happy?" he asked when he stalked back over.

It was then that I saw that the dog was staring at Wade—who'd gone up to the cage—with cautious eyes.

Hoax came to stand beside me, and we both stared as the two alpha males stared at each other.

"Do you want to…" the neighbor continued.

"Listen, Mags, we're a little busy right now. Do you think you can leave us alone?" Wade asked without once taking his eyes off the dog.

This "Mags" chick huffed and turned on her toe to walk away.

Neither man watched her go, but I did.

I also saw that she looked over her shoulder to see if either man had looked—they hadn't—and her eyes met mine.

She hesitated on the threshold of her duplex and narrowed her eyes.

I didn't look away, knowing that I couldn't or I'd risk losing ground—at least in her eyes—and waited her out.

It didn't take her long before she was rolling those beautiful eyes and stalking inside her place.

The door shut with a loud bang, which still didn't cause either man to look up.

"Tell me his story," Wade ordered.

I swallowed.

"The dog's name is Capo. He's seven years old. He retired from the military when he and his handler were in a Humvee that ran over a landmine. Capo was thrown free of the wreckage while the rest of his crew were caught in the flames or injured in the actual wreck." I paused. "He lost his rear leg and was placed with an adoptive family once he recovered—at least physically. The adoptive family couldn't get near him just like the vet couldn't. The only person able to get close was a wounded veteran who worked in the vet hospital in Germany. They'd hoped that his temper would calm once he no longer required to be caged, but it hasn't. I was brought in as a last resort before euthanasia."

Wade growled in anger as Hoax blew out a surprised breath.

"You think it's PTSD?" Hoax asked Wade and me.

"Could be," I admitted. "I've had MWD—military working dogs—before, but none of them were anywhere near this severe."

Hoax made a sound in his throat. Wade, on the other hand, went closer to the cage.

The dog's growl came back, but this time it was a low one instead of the high-pitched intense ones that were coming out of him before.

Honestly, this one was almost way more menacing than the first.

At least to me. Wade didn't seem to care.

He moved closer yet and pressed his palm flat against the cage, and the dog lunged at him.

I gasped and would've fallen straight on my ass if Hoax hadn't caught me around the waist.

"Easy, darlin'," he ordered. "It's all right."

I didn't see how…but the dog wasn't lunging and snarling anymore. He was sitting there staring at Wade's hand—which was still exactly where it'd been moments before—like he'd like to have it for breakfast.

"He's been fed," I felt it prudent to point out. "I fed him a burger and some fries from my lunch on the way home from Oklahoma."

Hoax snorted.

Wade looked over at me with laughter shining in those eyes that I loved.

"Duly noted," he rumbled. "Hoax, grab the cage with me?"

Luckily the cage had handles on the outside so there wasn't a need to grab the wire of the cage itself, reducing the possibility of Capo getting some little hors-d'oeuvres to hold him over until dinnertime.

Each man carried the cage on one side, and it took everything I had to ask Wade if he needed help.

He was limping badly—much worse than he had been three days ago—and that scared the crap out of me after hearing what I had heard from Bayou today.

Biting my lip, I closed the van door and reached into the driver's side—which still stood wide open—to grab for my purse, keys, and phone.

Once I had them, I hurried and rushed in front of the two men, throwing Wade's door wide open for them both to slip through.

Wade directed them to the living room, and it was then that I took in Wade's house for the first time.

It was barren, almost as if he hadn't planned to live there long.

As if he was always planning on coming back and didn't want to put down roots in case he had to pack his shit and go.

I felt a wave of shame roll over me as I thought about how I'd done this to him—and myself.

God, sometimes I felt like the biggest jerk in the world.

But I'd always been one of those people that reacted first and thought about the repercussions later, and unfortunately, I couldn't change that—it was too deeply ingrained in me.

"Put it down," Wade ordered.

Hoax did, groaning slightly when he stood up.

"We're just two peas in a pod, aren't we?" Wade laughed. "You with your broken ribs and arm, me with my leg."

Hoax grunted an affirmative and dropped down heavily on the couch only to lean forward and rip his leather jacket off. Or, at least, he tried to. The jacket got stuck on his cast and he was shaking it to get it off.

I laughed at his plight and moved forward, taking the cuff of the arm and tugged it gently free.

"Thanks," he said as I righted the armholes and laid it gently on the side of the couch.

"Welcome," I said as I joined him on the couch.

Then we both watched as Wade talked to the dog.

"How did he get in here?" Wade asked. "I'd like to take him out, but he doesn't have a collar on."

I sighed. "He was under sedation," I murmured. "And they got him in there after the fact. I didn't think about getting a collar on him, but they did give me the medication that they use to calm him down enough to take him outside and stuff. It's right here."

I pulled the bottle out of my purse and set it down on the card table that acted as a coffee table.

"We'll use that as a last resort," Wade suggested.

I didn't agree or disagree.

In fact, I was fairly sure that I was way over my head in this situation.

A text message alerted from my phone, and I absently pulled it up to my face and read it.

Kourt: Found a new place. It's in the Red-Light district.

I rolled my eyes at Kourt's words.

The 'Red-Light' district was actually a part of the city that had a traffic light every sixty yards for about two miles straight. It was a nice area, but it was residential and there was absolutely no reason for eighteen red lights in that two-mile stretch.

The rich people of Bear Bottom had built it that way to keep normal people from taking that route as a shortcut—which they had before—to the interstate.

Now, everyone avoided it at all costs, otherwise, it would add ten minutes to your commute instead of taking away ten minutes if you went the other way.

I texted him back with a smile on my face.

Landry: *You're going to hate driving to work from there.*

The last three days I'd used wisely.

After asking Kourt to leave, I'd then helped him pack as he'd searched for a place to stay.

Kourt: *True, but it's halfway through the lights, and I found a back way that nobody but the residents of the Red-Light district know about. No, I won't tell you what it is. Also, the house is furnished and move-in ready. I took the boxes this morning while you were driving. You're officially by yourself again.*

"Who are you texting?" Wade asked.

I looked up to find him staring at me instead of the dog.

"Kourt," I told him truthfully. "He moved out."

Something weird happened to Wade's face.

He looked almost…hopeful. Well, in reality, he looked too afraid to be hopeful. Cautiously hopeful maybe.

The dog whined then, and I perked up. "Whining's a good sound."

Wade looked back at the dog, who was staring at him with curiosity.

Inadvertently, Wade had moved away from the cage when he'd turned to ask me who was texting, and when he'd heard me say that Kourt had moved out, he'd completely turned his back on Capo.

And now Capo was staring at Wade as if he didn't like not being his center of attention.

"Sorry, Capo," Wade rumbled. "Where were we?"

Hoax turned the TV on at one point and I sat cross-legged on the couch, alternating my gaze from the TV—Hoax was literally watching *So You Think You Can Dance*—and watching Wade as he talked to the dog.

At one-point Wade had gotten comfortable on the floor next to the cage, his back leaning against the recliner, which was shoved up against the wall.

Wade spoke softly—too softly for me to hear over the television that Hoax had blaring—and Capo's eyes never once strayed from Wade.

At least not until I stood up to go to the bathroom.

His eyes met mine, and he narrowed them.

"It's okay," I said to the dog. "I just have to go to the bathroom. I'm not going to come close to you."

The dog dropped his head to his forepaws, but still didn't take his eyes off me as I walked away.

After finding the bathroom and using it, I wandered back into the main room.

The duplex was small, and the kitchen was directly off the living room. There was a small kitchen island separating the two, and on the island was some paperwork that caught my eye.

Admission papers.

"Wade, what's this?" I asked as I picked up the papers and started to read.

"Admission papers for the hospital tonight," he said from across the room.

My heart started to pound. "You're doing it tonight?"

Something in my voice must've alerted him to my state of mind, because he frowned. "Yeah. Why?"

I felt my heart start to palpitate.

"How are you so calm?" I wondered.

I wouldn't be.

Hell, I was freaking out, and it wasn't even my leg coming off!

"Because it's what I have to do." He paused. "And they're only keeping me overnight. Once the antibiotics are done, I'm free to go home. They're just ones they have to administer from the hospital and not something I can do at home."

And then I understood why he wasn't freaking out.

They weren't amputating his leg today like I'd feared. They were giving him IV antibiotics.

Shit.

I pressed my hand over my heart and realized that in my worried state, I'd clenched the papers in a tight fist.

Putting them down on the counter, I smoothed them out and pushed them to the center of the island. That was when I saw a balled-up piece of pink paper with girly handwriting on it.

I frowned and picked that up, too.

Tiffy. 883-3039.

I threw it into the trash.

He wouldn't be needing that.

Wade's chuckle had me looking at him.

His eyes were on the trash can where I'd just thrown Tiffy's number away.

"That was the nurse I have to talk to when I get to the hospital," he explained, making me feel dumb.

I winced and bent over to pluck the paper out of the trash can, and then put the paper back on top of the other papers that I'd practically ruined.

Once done with that, I took a seat at the kitchen island and tried to figure out what I should do next.

I wanted to stay where I was. I wanted to go with him to the hospital. I wanted to have him move back in with me. I wanted to wrap my arms around him and bury my face into his chest. I wanted to remember what it felt like to wake up beside him.

I wanted him back.

Which was comical since I was the one who made him leave.

The metal latch on the cage rattled, and my head snapped up just in time to see Wade opening the smaller of the two doors. It was designed to where you could open up a side hatch and deposit food or possibly a chew toy for the dog to play with without actually opening the entire cage and risk the dog getting out.

It was a good setup, and I was glad that I'd made the hefty purchase.

I watched, heart in my throat, as Wade's hand slowly eased inside the cage.

The dog didn't growl. Didn't move a single inch.

Capo did flinch when Wade's hand came near his big body, but otherwise he showed no outward appearance that he cared that Wade's hand was nearly touching him.

Wade didn't make the final move, though.

He waited, hand rock steady, inches away from him.

Finally, after what felt like fifteen minutes but was more likely three or four, Capo shifted until his back was pressing against Wade's hand.

I breathed in deeply as tears came to my eyes.

The dog wasn't a lost cause.

I knew it.

CHAPTER 12

Any pencil can be a number two pencil if you eat it.

-Wade to Landry

Wade

Running late, I parked my bike in the hospital parking lot and got off, hurrying as fast as my broken body could move without actually making agony jolt through me with every step.

I hadn't intended to spend the afternoon trying to get a dog to like me, but something in Capo had sparked a protective instinct in me. I also hated seeing my wife cry.

Always had.

Which led me to now, five minutes late for an appointment that was necessary to me hopefully keeping my leg.

Papers in hand, I walked onto the floor and looked for the nurses' station, finding it in the very center of the huge floor.

My eyes scanned the nurses that were all giving me their full attention.

"I'm looking for Tiffy," I rumbled.

A woman stood up and started toward me, her face the only one in the entire bunch that looked disinterested in me.

I was used to women's eyes being on me. One, because I was a police officer and being a police officer usually drew peoples' attention to me. Two, because I had my dad's genes. Tall, dark, and handsome—or so I'd been told.

Tiffy was a cute little thing. She was a short, slightly built woman with features that clearly hinted at Japanese ancestry.

"You are Wade?" she asked in a no-nonsense voice.

I nodded once. "That's me."

"You're late," she said.

I nodded. "I had a problem I had to deal with. I apologize."

Tiffy—who didn't look much like a Tiffy—narrowed her eyes. "Follow me. Your room is at the back of the floor."

I did and grinned when I realized she wasn't lying. The room really was in the back—and I meant way back.

It was also about three-quarters of the way through a remodeling process and likely wasn't supposed to have any patients in it.

"I doubt that we'll come check on you much once we get this started. The doctor said that you weren't in need of our attention, and honestly, I can't spare the manpower. We didn't have room for another patient, and you in this room that isn't even finished being remodeled goes to show that." She showed me to the bed. "I don't need you to change out of your clothes. I see that you're in the sleep pants that the doctor recommended. Good. All I'll need is your shirt off."

I tossed my phone, wallet, and keys onto the bedside table and then kicked off my tennis shoes.

Once those were off, I took my shirt off and turned to sit on the bed.

Tiffy—whose nametag read Greta—a name that still didn't fit her—walked in front of me and examined my arms.

"Left or right?" she questioned.

Her abrupt manner had me almost smiling.

I shrugged. "Left, I guess. I'm right-handed."

She moved to my left hand and examined it. "Don't even need a tourniquet."

My lip twitched. "No, probably not."

She put one on anyway and started an IV within seconds.

Moments after that, she directed me onto the bed. "I hope that your phone works, or that you're tired. The television in here doesn't work. We have two of these bags to run through you tonight. When this one is empty, I'll come hang the other bag. It should be about eight hours of flow. Any questions?"

After getting a negative shake of the head, she did some fancy things with the iPad on the bedside table and scanned the antibiotics barcode followed shortly by the hospital bracelet I'd gotten at the doctor's office earlier that morning.

She then hung up the meds—that had to have been in here waiting for me since I hadn't seen her carry anything back with her—and got me started.

Once I was hooked up, she directed me to lay back.

"You can go to the bathroom. You can get up and walk around if you so please. You can also come to the nurses' station if you need something to drink—but I really don't have any time to spare. I have thirty patients and four nurses so…"

I was understanding exactly what she was saying.

I'd been fit in, and by being fit in, I'd have to make do with the accommodations.

"Fine with me," I shrugged.

Tiffy nodded once. "Good. If you start to feel poorly, or you think something's wrong, you'll have to call the cell number that was given to you. Or yell. Yelling will likely get you a slower response though since we can't really hear you all the way back here. Any questions?"

"No, ma'am," I denied.

She narrowed her eyes. "All right, well, see you in about four hours, hopefully."

With that, she turned and left, but came to an abrupt halt when she nearly ran face first into Landry.

"Oh, sorry. Didn't see you there," Tiffy said to Landry.

Landry gave her a small smile. "It's okay. I didn't mean to sneak in or anything."

Tiffy waved it away. "These floors they have down to keep the ones beneath from being ruined are magical. I need to get some put in at my own place to keep my dog's wanderings in the middle of the night from waking me up. Bye."

With that she skirted around Landry and left, leaving us both watching each other in surprise.

"Abrupt, isn't she?" Landry teased.

I grinned. "A little bit."

I wouldn't ask what she was doing here.

I knew why she was there, just as well as I knew why I'd wanted to ask her to come with me and didn't.

I loved her, and I wanted her to be with me.

It didn't matter whether I was at home watching TV, at a club party, or in the damn hospital getting IV antibiotics. I wanted her with me, and I wouldn't apologize for that.

"Come here," I ordered.

She did, walking farther into the room.

Stepping over the large extension cords and tools that were piled up in the middle of the room—it looked like the nurses had done a cursory effort to clean the room up before they'd allowed me in here—she came to my side.

Her eyes automatically looked around the room, and she frowned.

"I was going to stay, but there's not a chair to sit in—not even one of the uncomfortable ones." She looked so forlorn that it took me a lot longer to come up with a solution than it probably should have.

"Sit with me," I said. "The bed's big enough."

She looked pointedly at the really small bed—at least it was 'small' when I was in it.

I was not a small man by any means, but we'd made it work before.

"Come on," I urged, scooting over until I was on the very edge. It left her about ten inches to lay her body—and even more, if she draped herself over me. "We've done this before."

Her eyes lit, and a smile curved up the corner of her mouth. "We have, haven't we?"

Yes, we had.

It'd been one very memorable camping trip.

As she dropped all of her stuff on the table next to mine and shed the t-shirt she was wearing that left her in only a camisole, I started to talk about my memories.

"My favorite thing about that night was your hair..."

***

"Omg, this was the worst idea ever!" Landry cried from the seat behind me.

I turned and looked at her over my shoulder, nearly choking when I saw what she was referring to.

Her hair had been wet before she'd left the house, and since the helmet had covered the top of her head, it was still damp. The bottom of her hair, however, was not.

Now, looking at her without the helmet on, I nearly laughed.

The top of her hair was curly from about her ears up. Now, the bottom? Well, it was straight as a board from the wind whipping through it on our five-hour bike ride.

"Don't laugh," she growled.

I held up my hands in surrender. "I'm sorry. It'll never happen again."

She rolled her eyes and tried to smooth the hair into something presentable, but ultimately decided that she would just put it up into a bun on the top of her head. Which, I had to agree was likely the best option at that point in time. Without a way to wet her hair down and start over, it was going to stay in its weird state.

And, seeing as we were at an open field without any water whatsoever, she wasn't going to be fixing it any time soon.

"Ready?" I asked.

"Ready, Freddy," she confirmed.

I pinched her ass and led her up to the bonfire, saying hi to a few friends I hadn't seen in a while, and introducing Landry to them as I passed.

"How do you know all these people?" she asked warily.

I'd invited her to an MC party, and she'd instantly agreed. But as she was looking around the area and seeing all the wild bikers drinking and having a good time, I was sure that she hadn't realized what she was getting into.

I barely hid my smile and pulled her in close to my chest.

"I know some of 'em." I paused. "Like that guy right there chugging his beer? That's Casten Red. He's a member of the Uncertain Saints. That one over there in the corner with the woman draped all over him? He's a member of Free, though they're not an official motorcycle club. Once or twice a year we get together and have a big party. Multiple motorcycle clubs from all over the state show up."

She swallowed. "I've never been to anything quite so…rambunctious."

I snorted. "Don't worry, honey. You ain't seen nothin' yet."

Six hours later, everyone was tired, totally sated from the shared cooking, and well on the way to being ready to go to bed.

Which was why I'd pulled the sleeping bag out of my saddlebags.

Landry looked at me warily. "Uhhh, what are you doing with that? And what the hell is it?"

I grinned and unzipped it, causing all the air to rush in and inflate the bag.

"It's a vacuum bag that I sucked all the air out of when I got my sleeping bag in there," I paused. "Otherwise it wouldn't have fit into my saddlebags."

Her smile grew as she looked around and saw a lot of the other people doing the same. "We're gonna sleep here in the middle of the field?"

I nodded and pulled the sleeping bag out of the vacuum bag and then unrolled it next to my bike. "Sure are."

Her smile was bright then. "I don't know why I'm so excited about sleeping on the ground, but I am."

Grinning, I bent down to unzip the bag and tossed it to the side. "Take off your pants and shoes and climb in."

She looked around the immediate area and frowned.

"Don't worry, baby. They're all doing the same thing you are." He paused. "And it's so dark that they're not going to see a thing."

Biting her lip, Landry followed my directions, starting with first her boots and then her pants. She did it so fast, though, that even I could barely see her.

"You could've at least given me a small show," I teased.

She giggled, making my heart lighten. "I'll remember that for next time...your turn."

I went about getting undressed much more slowly than her, and by the time I was laying on the sleeping bag next to her and zipping her up, I was horny as hell and needing her.

Having her zipped up so tight next to me was making my heart and other things do funny things.

"We're not doing it right here in the middle of a field surrounded by a hundred other people..."

"No?" I teased, pulling her lithe body closer.

When I did, she could clearly feel my erection, and it wasn't lost on me that her nipples were hard as diamonds.

"No," she whispered, sounding like she was trying to convince herself she meant no rather than convincing me.

"Okay," I murmured, twisting her so that she was back to my front, and my cock was pressed up tight to her ass crack. "We'll just go to sleep then."

We stayed like that for long minutes, and not once did her body calm down enough to relax. She wanted me just as much as I wanted her…there was no doubt in my mind. I just had to wait patiently…

A small moan pierced the quiet of the night, and I knew that I wasn't the only one in the entire field who was on the verge of getting some.

***

"That was the worst ten minutes of my life," Landry whispered. "I wanted you so freakin' bad, but I was fighting my every instinct. The mere idea of having sex with you in that field made my blood run hot…but my brain said that I shouldn't do it…shouldn't want it."

"But you did," I paused. "And it was hearing all those other people quietly doing it, too, that finally convinced you."

She shivered against my side, and I felt my cock stiffen even further.

The loose sleep pants that I wore were doing nothing to conceal the erection that was tenting the front of my pants.

Landry tried to ignore it, but there really was no ignoring the thing. It bounced and bobbed with each beat of my heart, causing her to laugh.

It always had.

She liked that my dick had a mind of its own.

She also liked to play with me—to torture me—just because she was so fascinated by it.

Her favorite thing in the world was to order me 'not to get hard' and then play with my soft cock.

And, okay, who the hell wouldn't get hard with their wife's hand on their dick?

That's right, nobody.

But, I did try.

It usually took me thinking about an arrest that was particularly difficult or having to do something repugnant like cleaning vomit out of the back seat of my police cruiser, but I did manage to get about one to two minutes before I just couldn't take it anymore.

How did I know it was one to two minutes? I watched the clock while it happened.

"I want to touch it," she whispered, sounding tired.

I snorted. "Then do it."

Her eyes flicked to the door and back to my dick, which made it jerk.

"The nurse told me that she didn't have time or enough staff to check on me tonight," I said. "She flat out said that I'd need to call her if I had any problems, too. Trust me when I say, they won't be coming."

She looked torn for all of five seconds, and then lifted the waistband of my sweats up with one finger, peeking inside like it held a present for her and she just wanted to get a small peek.

That lasted for all of three seconds, and then she was pushing the band of my sweats down and over the length of my cock.

I growled a low curse and hissed when she moved the band even lower so that it was laying against my balls, causing my dick to stick straight up in the air with the added support. Not that it really needed the support, but still.

"If they come in here," she whispered. "I'm going to be so freakin' mad at you."

I reached for the little light switch on the bed, ignoring the way my goddamn leg screamed when I moved it and hit the switch.

The room around us plunged into darkness, and the only light there was to be had was the green glowing numbers on the remote control laying on the bedside table.

I'd just settled back into the bed, relief swamping me from no longer having any strain on my leg when I lost what little breath I'd been able to regain as her tiny hand closed around my dick.

It jumped in her hand, and my balls rode up even closer to my body, and I practically started to count in my head to keep myself from coming.

I could masturbate for a goddamn half hour while watching porn on my phone, but goddamn if one tiny little touch from her goddamn soft hand didn't bring me to my knees.

"What are you thinking about?" Her breath whispered across my lips, and I groaned.

"You," I said. "Your hand wrapped around me. The way you make me feel. The way that I can't seem to hold onto my control when you're anywhere around." I searched for her mouth with mine and found it when she closed the distance.

Our lips met in heated fervor, and I growled as her tongue slipped into my mouth.

I'd never been much of a kisser. I didn't like kissing—the goddamn mouth was a hot zone of bacteria and other things that really grossed me out—but Landry had always been the exception.

My tongue dueled with hers, and my gut clenched as I tried to tell myself not to come.

"Baby," I panted against her lips, pulling back only slightly. "Take those sweats off and get on top of me."

She did as I asked, moving with haste to do exactly what I'd asked of her.

Moments later, her hot pussy was settling down over the saddle of my hips, and my dick was in heaven.

A thought occurred to me, and I moved until I was on my side and she was directly in front of me, her back facing my front.

It put us in the perfect position for me to take her while also being covered up on the off chance that a nurse did decide to come check on us.

I hiked her leg up and curled my arm around her thigh.

"Put me inside of you," I ordered, sawing my cock back and forth between her exposed pussy lips.

By the time she reached for me, I was thoroughly coated in her juices, and I was yet again on the verge of coming.

My breaths were coming fast, and the feel of Landry's thigh in my hand had me thinking such naughty thoughts.

The skin right near her panty line was so goddamn soft that I wanted to rub my lips against it, make my beard give her a burn that said 'Wade's been here.'

But then she latched onto my cock and guided it to her entrance, and I lost the ability to think.

The only thing I was able to concentrate on was the way her tight pussy enclosed over my cock.

She reached for the blanket as I thrust inside of her hard, filling her up completely full without a second to think.

A squeak left her throat, and she threw her head back, narrowly missing slamming it into my chin.

I leaned forward and latched my teeth onto the cord of her neck and started to thrust into her roughly.

"Cover us up, baby," I ordered.

She blindly searched for the blanket that she'd dropped and yanked it over us—just in time, too.

Because moments after she pulled it up and settled it over both of our hips, a nurse's voice sounded from the hallway, causing both of us to freeze.

Seconds after that, my cock throbbing inside of her, the door pushed open as a woman started to speak.

"...Not sure if it's in here, but hell, I'll look. Oh, crap! I forgot it was in use...I'm so sorry! Do y'all, erm, need anything?" The nurse wasn't wearing the same colors as the other nurses I'd seen, so I assumed she was a student.

"No," Landry sounded tired, drugged. "We're fine. He's doing great. I hope you don't mind, but I had to use the bed since there wasn't a chair."

"No, not at all," the girl smiled. "I can bring you one."

Landry waved it away. "We're okay right now. When I'm ready to have some room to myself, I'll come ask for one."

The woman smiled. "Okay...you can go back to sleep now."

"Thank you," Landry cheerfully replied.

All the while she was holding an intelligent conversation, I wondered what in the hell it was going to take for the woman to go the hell away.

I was literally dying, and all the while she was talking, Landry was squeezing things inside of her.

And then the door was closed, and I couldn't help it. I ruthlessly fucked her, barely waiting long enough for the door to close behind the woman.

And then I was coming, and Landry was, too.

I immediately hated myself when my leg's throbbing finally overcame the euphoria.

"I love you, Landry," I whispered into her ear, trying not to relay how much pain I was in. "And I'm glad that you came tonight."

She laughed. "Was that literally, or you know" —clenching herself around me— "literally?"

I snorted and pulled out of her, loving the small cry that left her lips. "Both, baby. Both."

It wasn't until two hours later that our perfect little world was shattered.

Hoax was whispering furiously into the phone, and I had to start him over twice to understand what he was saying.

"Someone just burned Landry's place to the ground."

With those eight words, our worlds changed.

CHAPTER 13

I doubt whiskey is the answer, but it's worth a shot.

-T-shirt

Wade

"You're doing an excellent job, and you've not received any complaints from anyone per se…"

My brows lifted, and I waited for the chief to continue.

"However, I'm getting feedback from your officers that you're intimidating and hard to work with," the chief finished.

I blinked once then felt my lips twitch before I took pity on the chief and replied, "I can either pass a drug test or keep being me…it's completely up to you which one of those you choose."

The chief rolled his eyes.

"You're making them sweat, and this should be a more comfortable environment to work in than you're making it. All I'm asking is that you dial it back a bit and allow them to do their jobs without pissing them off," he continued as if I hadn't just said that it would take me doing drugs for me to be nice to them.

I frowned. "If you're talking about Watson and Peterson, I really can't help what I did. They were in the wrong."

The chief sat back in his seat, causing the leather to creak and the plastic to strain as his big bulk stretched the limits of the weight capacity.

The chief was a big man and definitely wouldn't be able to pass the department's physical any longer.

Really, none of them would.

"Tell me what they did that was so wrong," the chief ordered.

I crossed my arms over my chest as well, mimicking his stance.

"They tried to get out of their physical test by bribing the physical education teacher that we use through the high school. I caught them in the act while out at the course, teasing the shit out of the teacher. Bayou was there if you don't believe me," I explained.

Really, what Peterson and Watson had done was harass the shit out of her, and if Bayou hadn't happened to be out in the parking lot waiting for me to go to lunch with him, he might not have heard what was going on and been able to intervene.

The woman looked goddamn scared, to be honest.

I didn't like when women looked scared.

Hell, Bayou had been utterly pissed.

If I hadn't come out when I had, Bayou would've likely slammed his fist into both of their throats.

The chief sighed. "I understand, but to be honest, half the men in this department can't pass that test. It's an impossible feat for an everyday officer. We're not all Navy SEALS." I nearly rolled my eyes at that.

He would say that.

Especially considering he was one of the ones that couldn't pass it.

Lucky for him, people on desk duty no longer had to pass physicals. They implemented that requirement after he'd already passed his physical before he became the chief.

They only had to pass the psychological tests once every six months.

"Listen," I said. "Until that changes, I have no choice but to follow the rules."

The chief sighed. "Which brings us back around to what I really needed to talk to you about. You're officially on desk duty until your leg is healed. I know you wanted to come back, but since you yourself couldn't run the course, we're no longer able to keep you on patrol."

I felt my stomach bottom out. Being on desk duty was the worst form of torture. But, I'd also heard it from my sergeant the day before, so it wasn't that much of a shock.

I'd be relegated to desk duty at the front desk, and I'd have to actually talk to the public who came into the department with their petty little complaints. I don't actually hate doing it, but I so wanted to be back doing the job that I loved.

"I *can* pass the test," I pointed out.

And I could.

Despite my leg being in pain, I could—and did—pass the test.

"I know that you ran it this morning to prove a point to the other officers," the chief sighed. "But you haven't been cleared by the doctor, and as per department policy, you have to have that to be cleared for active duty."

I growled low in my throat. "I can do the job."

I *needed* to do the job.

Having to deal with petty crime reports would literally kill me.

"That may be true," my chief agreed, sounding tired. "But until you're back on your feet officially, and have a release from a doctor, you're on desk duty. You're also on vacation for the next two weeks. Go home."

Knowing when I wasn't going to get what I wanted, I stood. "Fine. But don't expect me to be nice to these people that come in here thinking that they're gonna play tattle on Tommy, their neighbor who let their dog shit on their lawn."

With that, I left the chief's office and went out to my truck, annoyed all over again that my officers were a bunch of pussies.

I knew when I signed up to be the sergeant of all these little twits that it was going to be tough. I just didn't realize how tough.

God, they were the whiniest bunch of grown men I'd ever had to deal with.

To make matters worse, I was supposed to return to work in two days before meeting with the chief. Now I have two more weeks before I can return.

It'd been a week since Hoax had called to tell us that Landry's place—the one that we'd built when we were three months into our marriage—had burned to the ground.

And during that time, we hadn't made any progress in finding out who did it. At this point, we were leaning toward a gaggle of teenagers that'd been caught setting fires to mailboxes a few streets down from our home.

But, after listening to their confessions, I couldn't see them doing it.

They were scared and adamant that they hadn't been on that street.

Of course, if I'd heard that the house burned down after I had set the mailbox on fire, I would've denied it, too.

My gut, however, told me that there was something more going on than I was aware of, and I planned to find it out what it was.

Starting now, seeing as I was still on medical leave, I would have plenty of time to do whatever the fuck I wanted.

But first…I wanted to go see Landry.

Stopping by her favorite place to eat, I grabbed two street tacos and a basket of fries for her along with five street tacos and a basket of fries for me, and then headed to the daycare.

When I pulled up outside and shut the bike off, I marveled at how good it felt to be able to stop by here with lunch again. Hell, this used to be something I did almost daily seeing as I almost always got an hour for lunch, so why not spend that hour with her since she had to eat, too?

We'd take our lunches to the park bench across the street from the daycare, and we'd watch all the ducks swim and fish jump while we spoke about nothing and everything.

The wailing scream of an infant as the door to the daycare opened dragged me from my thoughts, and I stiffly got off my bike.

My leg—although not worse—certainly wasn't completely healed. But, it seemed the antibiotics were working since the infection had stopped spreading according to the doctor, so at least that was something.

He guesstimated that it would be about four more weeks until there was no more persistent pain, and about six weeks until I could return to light exercise.

"Hey, man." I turned to find Bayou waving.

I gave him a wave back, but he didn't stop and neither did I, both of us on our own missions.

He was dressed for work—he was the warden at a medium-security prison just outside of town—and looked like he was in a hurry.

Snatching up the food bags from my saddlebags, I waved to the woman who was obviously taking her sick kid home—the vomit on the kid's shirt was a dead giveaway—and headed inside.

I found my wayward woman in the kitchen washing her hands. Her sad, brown paper-bagged lunch sat on the counter next to a bottle of half-finished water.

She looked tired today.

Although that was probably because I'd kept her up late doing things to her that I hadn't been able to do in quite a long time…such as rolling over and lifting her leg in the middle of the night and taking her.

"Hey," I called out softly.

Landry's head snapped up, and a wide smile filled her face. "Hey! What are you doing here?"

I sighed as I remembered exactly why I was there. "My chief said that I was taking my bad mood out on all the officers under my command and that I needed to take another two weeks mandatory medical leave to get my head on straight so that I was in the right frame of mind before I came back to work for desk duty."

She snickered. "Oh, I bet you just loved hearing that."

I rolled my eyes and gestured to the bag with a tilt of my chin. "You have time to eat some lunch with me?"

Landry grabbed her lunch and stuck it in the fridge with what looked like the kids' afternoon snacks.

"Anything is better than a boring ol' sandwich," she teased.

I snorted. "I've been telling you that for years now."

She shrugged and batted her eyelashes at me. "Let me go tell Mindy I'm taking my lunch."

Landry dashed down the hall and I stopped at the office, placing our food on the desk while I searched for a cord to plug my phone in while we were eating.

My hand hit the mouse, and I glanced at the computer.

Facebook was pulled up, and Landry's Old Dogs New Tricks Rescue page was up, and the browser tab was blinking indicating she'd gotten a new message or notification.

Landry found me digging through her drawers.

"It's plugged into the wall by the filing cabinet," she said, gesturing toward the corner.

I saw the cord and went for it while saying, "You got a message."

I felt her move behind me, her ass brushing mine as I bent over and reached for the cord on the ground.

Grinning, I plugged my phone in and placed it on the cabinet before turning around.

My eyes went to Landry's angry face, and I stilled.

"What's wrong?" I asked as I got a good look at her face.

Landry's eyes flicked up to me, and she threw her arms up in the air and gestured at the computer, a disgusted look on her face. "When I first found out about Capo, there was this other chick who wanted him as well. Unfortunately, my qualifications and accommodations, as well as experience with working with abused animals, made me better qualified to take the dog. The woman was pissed, and she hasn't stopped harassing me on Facebook since. I've blocked her twice, but she just makes a new profile with a different email address and bam, the harassment starts all over again. Since my dog rescue page is public, anyone can message me. But it's getting to the point where I'm running out of options, and I don't know what else to do."

I moved to where I could see the screen and read the messages, feeling my shoulders get tighter and tighter at the venom in the woman's words.

"Why is she so mad?" I asked in confusion, setting the phone back down on the counter.

"She's mad because apparently her son, who was in the military and is now wheelchair-bound due to the injuries he sustained, wanted the dog. That's all I have," she explained.

"Huh," I paused. "What was the first name she talked to you under?"

Landry did some clicking and then maneuvered herself into her list of blocked people. It was quite a hefty list.

"Are these all her?" I questioned.

"Yep," she said. "If they come to my other box, I normally just block them straight away. But this time she was smart and started in with a short story about her dog that she wanted to see about getting hospice care for. Once she had my attention, she switched to ranting about what an awful person I was for stealing a dog away from a veteran."

"This was the first name she messaged me from." Landry pointed to a name.

I crossed back to my phone and shot a quick text to a buddy who was good with finding shit on people and then touched the top of Landry's ear. "Let's go eat, baby. We'll worry about this later, okay?"

She sighed and stood up. "Sure. I hope you got me extra sauce. You know I like it hot."

The look I gave her caused her cheeks to flush.

I bared my teeth. "I know you like it hot, darlin'."

She pinched my ass as we walked out of the front door but stopped to talk to the lady manning the counter. She was new, and I'd never met her before.

"We'll be back, Tammy."

We were halfway through lunch when I got my first hit on the name that Landry had given me.

Unfortunately, since my phone was still charging in Landry's office, I didn't realize that I had something until I was already halfway home because a second call came through.

What I learned from that phone call had been very, very disturbing.

CHAPTER 14

Why are iPhone chargers not called 'Apple Juice?'

-Landry's secret thoughts

Landry

I glared at the man who was currently sitting his ass in my car as I was on the verge of leaving for work.

"Wade, get out!" I growled in frustration.

"I'm going with you," he replied stubbornly. "There's no argument here. I still own half the daycare, so there's no reason in hell that I can't be there with you. And I get bored. Seriously, please take pity on me."

Then he rolled his lip over and gave me those sad, pouty-faced eyes, and I melted.

"Fine," I growled. "But you have to do the same thing there that you would have to do at home. No walking around. No heavy lifting. No nothing. You sit in the chair and be good."

Wade rolled his eyes but nonetheless agreed with a sigh.

"You promise?" I pushed.

He held up three fingers and said, "Scout's Honor."

We were halfway to the daycare—at five-thirty-five in the morning to allow me to open by six—when I took a detour for a bag of donut holes.

"You want something?" I asked, getting out of the car before he could say a word.

He opened the door and got out, too, and I frowned.

"Wade, what the hell is going on?" I asked. "I've done this a million times before. I don't need you to—"

He cut me off with a kiss.

"Wade," I said when he finally pulled back. "Tell me what the hell is going on."

He looked down into my eyes and sighed. "Get your donuts, baby. Make sure you get me a kolache with sausage."

He watched me walk away, and honestly, I was surprised he'd even done that.

I hadn't been able to walk through the house without him following me over the last twelve hours.

Yesterday, before he'd left, he'd been acting normal. When he came back half an hour later with Capo in his cage and sat in his truck in the parking lot for the next three hours, I realized that something was wrong.

I didn't realize how wrong until he followed me to his home that I supposed I could call my own home now. Then he followed me through the house and had acted so freakin' weird that I'd almost snapped.

Luckily, we'd gone to bed early, and I let it go thinking he was just having an off day.

It wasn't until I was inside the donut shop and waiting for the kolache to heat up that I realized the reason he hadn't come into the donut store. There was no way that anybody would be hiding in here. It was all one big open room. You could see the donuts being made, fried and glazed. There were three employees total standing in various spots around the large room.

It was lit up like the Fourth of July, and the large plate glass windows made light spill out into the parking lot.

There wasn't a single freakin' thing that he couldn't see.

Sighing, I smiled at Jamal who gave me my donuts. "Have a good day, Landry. I packed an extra sausage kolache in there for the ex. I'm glad to see him with you again."

I blushed. "Thank you, Jamal. Have a wonderful day, too."

When we were back out in the car and I was pulling out of the parking lot, I turned my head slightly and regarded Wade.

"Tell me what's going on," I ordered again.

Wade remained silent for a little too long, and I turned my head facing forward.

"You're a mule-headed, stubborn ass who drives me insane," I growled. "I swear to God, this is one thing that I don't miss from us being married—your need to protect me from something while not sharing whatever that something was with me. Do you remember what happened when you tried to do that last time?"

My husband started to chuckle. That chuckle quickly died off his face when we arrived at the daycare and saw how dark it was outside.

"What's up with the lighting?" he asked, sounding suspicious.

"The last storm we had fried 'em," I explained. "I keep meaning to get them replaced, but since the sun's like ten minutes away, and we don't open for another twenty, it hasn't bothered me enough to make me actually remember to make the call."

"I don't like you opening this place up in the dark," he growled.

I rolled my eyes heavenward, praying for patience.

"Wade, seriously. I swear to God," I growled. "Tell me what's going on!"

He grunted and got out of the truck, rounding the hood to come to my side and help me out.

I rolled my eyes and took his hand.

"I'm going to have to leave around mid-morning to run to the house and let Capo out before my therapy appointment," he said as he walked us to the door. Once there, he unlocked it with keys from his own pocket and easily input the alarm code before flicking on the lights. From that point he left me where I stood to go check out the various rooms, clearing them of anything bad.

It wasn't until he came back and gave me a funny look that I frowned.

"What?"

"The lights are out in the back play area, too?"

I nodded. "They are. The electrician said it was most likely that they were all on the same breaker. He offered to fix it…for a lot of money. I wasn't going to use ten grand to replace lights when I don't actually have that much readily available."

He narrowed his eyes. "He gave you a price of ten grand?"

I nodded. "He did."

He growled. "Who did you use?"

After telling him, I went about getting the rooms ready for the day and then made my way to the front largest room where all the early arrivals would hang out until the teachers started to arrive at eight.

For the first two hours of the day, they were all mine, and that was why I started to stuff my face full of my donuts so I didn't have to share.

All the while Wade watched me.

"If you're going to stare at me like I'm in danger, you need to tell me why," I pushed. "Because all it's really doing is pissing me off."

His lips twitched. "I know how to smooth down your hackles, darlin'."

I rolled my eyes.

He did, but that wasn't the point now, was it?

"I'll tell you…after I have more information." He paused. "After the incident happened last year…was anything said?"

The 'incident' he was referring to was nearly a tragedy.

The definition of a tragedy is an event that has caused great suffering.

And that was the perfect word to describe that hellish day last year.

It'd been the one and only time since we'd divorced that I'd wished that I could have slept in Wade's arms.

That morning, I'd come to work as per my usual. One of my first babies that arrived—or should have arrived—didn't show. Her sister did, though. At the same time, I'd had a new mother who was dropping off her three-year-old triplets that were starting that day, so I hadn't thought to question why the sister had arrived, but the baby sister hadn't. Automatically assuming that she was sick, I'd gone about my business until about two o'clock when the dad came to pick the babies up.

Except, there was only one baby to pick up.

The other, I'd explained to him, had never been brought in.

After having a pretty good freak-out on me, so much so that I'd been forced to call the cops—which was when Wade showed up on the scene—it was discovered that the mother didn't bring the baby after viewing the tapes from the state-of-the-art camera system that Wade had recommended I get.

And thank God I did, or that baby would've been in her mother's car even longer.

Because it came out later that the mother had been flustered. Her older daughter had thrown a fit, and when the little sister—who was eighteen months—would've normally followed them inside, she'd instead taken a detour to the back of the car. Then, when she realized her mother's car door was still open, she'd climbed back inside the car and curled up on the floor and fallen back to sleep.

All the while, I thought the little girl was with mom, and the mom thought the little girl was with me.

Meanwhile, the little girl was in a covered parking garage, but still in quite a bit of heat.

The girl had lived, but she'd suffered minor brain damage from the incident.

"What do you mean was anything said?" I asked.

He gave me a look that I knew meant he was getting irritated. "Was anything said by the mother?"

Oh.

"Well, yes," I replied. "She was quite justifiably upset, and she did say some pretty mean things to me. She started to harass the daycare. Leaving bad reviews on the daycare's Facebook page and stuff like that. Bad Yelp reviews. But, since this town is on the smaller side, everyone knew what happened. And, since you told me to release the video camera footage, it wasn't like she could refute me."

He grunted. "I'm still pissed about that."

I was, too.

I was even more pissed that that little girl had suffered so needlessly.

It was so fucking easy for a young child to get lost in the confusion. They were so curious by nature, and their natural instinct was to push the limits—and by doing what she did best, being curious, it had almost cost her her life.

"That day, when that dad pushed you accusing you of losing his kid? I nearly lost my shit," Wade rumbled. "Then the mother came, screeching in on her little mini-van tires trying to sling accusations at you while their daughter sat in her rear floorboards unconscious? I wanted nothing more than to beat the shit out of both of them." He paused. "Never wanted to punch a woman before, but then and there? Yeah, I sure the fuck would have if I knew that I would get away with it."

I snorted.

"But anyway, other than just small stuff—petty little things here and there—I haven't actually heard from her in well over two months. Which is a record. When the kids need picked up or dropped off, grandma does it," I explained.

His eyes went wide. "The kids still come here?"

I nodded. "I'm the only daycare in town. Plus, after that happened, both parents decided to get a divorce. I think right now dad is living at grandma's house, and mom doesn't have much to do with them except for on her scheduled days."

"You mean to tell me that dad got custody because mom's a nutjob." He snorted. "Seems like the kids would be better off with grandma with both of those people as their parents."

I smiled.

Just as I was about to reply, my first kiddo arrived.

"Hello there, Darrow!" I sang, holding my hands out.

Darrow's mother stopped long enough to hand me Darrow's diaper bag, a half-finished bottle, and a check for this week's tuition which she was three days late with. "Sorry. Gotta go. Bye."

With that, she left, and I sighed.

"She's like twelve minutes early," Wade pointed out as he watched Darrow's mother speed away.

"I normally leave the lights off and keep the door locked until six o'clock exactly. With you here, I didn't remember to do that," I explained.

He grunted. "Tomorrow we'll keep the door locked then. What time does Darrow's mother get here in the afternoon?"

I sighed. "Six, if we're lucky. Sometimes six-thirty."

"Fuck," he rumbled. "What a life to have. I'll bet he has more of an attachment to you and his teachers than he does his own mother. How old is he?"

"Six months," I murmured. "And there was this one time that I was holding Darrow and the mom came to pick him up early for some reason. When I went to hand him over, Darrow threw an unholy fit. The mom stormed out, leaving him here, and didn't come back to pick him up until after closing time."

He snorted. "What exactly did she expect would happen when she leaves him here for twelve hours a day?"

I shrugged. "Unfortunately, some parents don't have that luxury. They have to work. I'm here to love them while they're busy."

I dropped a kiss on Darrow's forehead, and then walked him into the main room and placed him on the floor next to some toys.

All the while, I felt Wade's eyes on me like a hot brand.

When I stood up once more, I turned to find him still staring, totally transfixed.

"What?" I whispered.

His eyes slipped from my ass to my face, and he smiled sadly. "I was just thinking that our babies would've been beautiful."

My heart lurched into my throat. "Yeah." I looked down at my hands. "They would have."

***

Twelve hours later I was climbing into Wade's truck this time after he had switched vehicles after letting Capo out. My heart lurched into my throat when I saw Capo in the back seat, unrestrained, staring at me like I was an interloper that he wanted to deal with.

Capo had come a long way from the first day that I'd met him. He was now able to come out of the cage for extended periods of time as long as Wade was around. Capo was also able to go outside for short walks with a muzzle.

I wasn't aware that we were quite that far along, though.

I swallowed hard. "Uhhhh, Wade?"

Wade's smile was quick and only half-hearted.

I sighed and settled into my seat, buckling my seatbelt while I kept my mouth shut.

He'd gotten call after call, text after text, and generally got into a progressively worse mood as the day had gone by.

Needless to say, I wasn't very happy with the way this day had gone, and Wade wasn't even apologizing for keeping something from me.

I was so frustrated, in fact, that I didn't even realize that we weren't headed home until we pulled up outside Bayou's house.

And we weren't the only ones there. All the boys from the club were standing outside, on Bayou's front lawn, in a loose circle. All of them wore their cuts—their MC leather vests that declared them Bear Bottom Guardians—and looked intimidating as hell.

My eyes searched the small cul-de-sac that Bayou lived on, and I saw that I wasn't the only one watching.

Nope, there was a young woman out on her front porch, sitting on her porch swing, drinking what appeared to be sweet tea. She was staring unrepentantly at the group, though her eyes followed Hoax as he split off from the loose circle of men and came out our way.

He winked at me as he opened my door, and it was then I realized that at some point while I'd been staring, Wade had exited the vehicle and gotten Capo out.

"Miss Landry." He winked.

I smiled at Hoax.

"Do you know why Wade's mad?" I blurted.

He was literally the only one out of the bunch who was wearing something besides a black t-shirt and blue jeans. He'd changed it up with a red shirt and blue jeans.

His arm flexed as he extended his open palm out to me.

"Can't say that I do," he answered. "He called us all here to explain, though, so maybe you'll only have a little bit longer to wait."

Lord, I hoped so.

A brooding Wade was an unhappy Wade, and anything other than a happy Wade was hard to be around.

I took Hoax's hand and dropped down from my husband's lifted truck.

The moment my feet were on the ground, I pulled away, which gave me a perfect view of the woman on the front porch across the street and her narrowed eyes aimed directly at me.

"You have a fan club," I told Hoax as I reached back inside the truck for my half-empty water bottle. "Do you know her?"

Hoax hummed in agreement. "She's the nurse that I saw last week when I went to the ER for something. I didn't know she lived there, otherwise I might've visited Bayou a whole hell of a lot sooner."

I snorted with barely contained laughter. "Something for your arm?"

His eyes went wonky for a second. "No."

It was so final that I realized he most certainly did not want to talk about his problem.

"Landry, baby. Come here."

Wade's lovely voice slid down my spine, and it took everything I had not to shiver.

Skirting around Hoax, I headed for Wade where he was standing in the loose circle, the one that had pushed out a little bit when Wade and I had arrived to allow us room to stand as well.

I swallowed as I met each man's curious eyes.

There were five men there in total.

Hoax—who was the most recent one that I'd met. Linc and Rome, who I'd never said anything more than hi to over the course of Wade's and my separation. Bayou, who gave me a warm welcoming smile. Ezekiel—better known as Zee—with his colorful tattoos. And finally, Castiel, a man who worked with my husband and who hadn't said a civil word to me since I'd left him.

I quickly looked away from that particular pair of eyes and smiled back at Bayou.

"You have a new injury since I saw you last," I commented.

There was a new laceration that was right underneath his left eye that looked like it hadn't felt really good to get considering the cut also had a large bruise surrounding it.

"Had a young man think it was okay to start a prison riot yesterday," he calmly replied. "I convinced him differently."

I snickered and leaned into Wade, who wrapped his arm around me and resituated his weight so that he could better accommodate me.

"Your hand looks good," Castiel said.

I felt my stomach sink.

I really, really didn't want to talk to Cass. He was the most welcoming in the beginning, but definitely the worst in the end.

"Yeah," I flexed it. "Still can't feel the back of my hand, though."

I didn't look him in the eye, and I felt Wade shift.

I looked up at him to see him frowning down at me.

"What?" I whispered.

He opened his mouth to reply, but Bayou interrupted him.

"So why are we here, Wade?" Bayou rumbled. "My fuckin' face hurts."

I snorted and turned back to see Bayou gently prodding the skin to the side of his hurt eye.

Meaning Bayou didn't want to be standing out talking when he could be ignoring everyone and everything.

Wade's gaze shifted down to me once more, then he sighed.

"Yesterday I was made aware that Landry was being harassed by a woman who was upset that Landry got Capo and she didn't," Wade started.

At the mention of Capo's name, the dog shifted his weight and leaned into Wade's other side. All attention turned to him for a few seconds and Capo started to growl.

Wade sighed, and I turned my face away, just as the others did.

"Anyway, I had Cass do some research into it, and he found out that that the original name she used was also the maiden name of a woman who takes her children to Landry's daycare," Wade continued.

I stiffened.

"Really?" Bayou asked, large arms crossing menacingly over his chest. "Who is it?"

"Her name is Deborah Shultz. The name she used originally to try to get Capo was Debbie Petty," Castiel said, making my eyes reluctantly turn to him.

"Deborah Shultz. Why does that sound so familiar?" Hoax asked.

"Deborah Shultz is the crazy chick who tried to blame Landry for losing her kid while the kid had been in her car—in the heat, in a parking garage—for six-plus hours," Bayou rumbled. "She's just fortunate that it wasn't one of our hundred degree days or the kid would be dead."

That surprised me that he remembered those details.

Though, I guess it shouldn't.

The Bear Bottom Guardians had a significant understanding of what happened in their community. Their fingers lay on the pulse of Bear Bottom, and if anything happened, they were the first to know. It didn't matter if ol' Mrs. Gable, the ninety-year-old Army nurse veteran had tried to shoot the delivery driver again, or if the young teenager who had always been sweet as pie had suddenly turned into a goth girl over the weekend.

They knew it, and nothing ever came as a surprise to them—at least not when I was around.

They were superhuman it seemed.

"Yep," Wade confirmed. "She wasn't smart using her maiden name. It was easy enough to track her."

"All the other names are phony as fuck," Castiel said.

"So, what do we do now?" I finally asked, still not meeting Castiel's eyes.

"We file a restraining order against her." Castiel's words startled me into making eye contact, and I felt my belly clench at the lack of warmness in his eyes. "You come up to the department tomorrow, and we'll get you squared away. I ran the info by the judge today, and he's already agreed to approve the order."

I swallowed hard. "Okay."

Wade's arm went around my waist, and I felt comforted by the solid warmth. "I'll get her up there in the morning around eleven. That's when she takes her lunch. Okay?"

Castiel nodded.

"What else aren't you telling me?" I finally asked. "You could've told me all of that earlier."

Wade sighed. "She's using your name and business to get dogs."

I blinked. "Okay…"

"And she's taking them somewhere," Castiel said. "But they never actually get to her house. She's not rehoming them. Honestly, it wouldn't surprise me that once she gets the dogs, she drops them off on an abandoned highway on the way home, because literally, nobody has seen her with any dogs."

I got a sick feeling in my stomach.

"She's using my name to get dogs, and then is doing something—likely something not so good—to them. And nobody can find them at all?" I repeated, making sure I understood him.

"And, on top of that, she's been taking in funds that were meant to be donated to you and your cause," Castiel continued. "There's like eight different fundraisers she's doing right now, promising that she's sending out t-shirts and stuff like that for donating…and hasn't done it yet. She raised over three grand with her last one, and some of the donors are starting to ask questions."

I let my head fall back on my neck, and I looked at the sky that was slowly starting to sink in the sky, dropping below the line of trees in the distance.

"Of course," I groaned. "I should've known when she stopped hounding me at work that she'd found some other way to vent her frustration with me."

"Just sayin'," Hoax drawled. "But I didn't think you did anything wrong."

"She didn't," Wade replied. "It was the mother's fault for not paying attention to whether her child actually followed her into the daycare, not Landry's fault. Sure, Landry could've asked, but it was a little chaotic that day with the three new triplets showing up. Furthermore, the mom sometimes let the grandmother watch the baby, so it wasn't all that unusual for only one kid to show up. How was she supposed to know that the baby's absence that day wasn't just a normal thing?"

I felt my heart start to warm at Wade's faith in me.

And, once again, I was reminded of how stupid and selfish I'd been when I filed for divorce.

"Bitch is crazy," someone said from behind us.

I whirled, my heart in my throat at having someone standing directly behind me, and smiled at Liner.

Liner was one of the only people, besides Bayou, to talk to me. He also didn't drop me like a hot potato when I'd done the unthinkable and filed for divorce.

"Hi, Liner," I murmured. "You're not talking about me, are you?"

He rolled his eyes and raised one hand to mess with my hair.

I slapped his hand away, causing him to laugh.

"I'm talking about ol' Debbie Doozy," he replied.

"Aren't you her neighbor?" Rome asked.

"Yeah," he replied. "It seems like I attract all the crazy neighbors."

He directed a look toward Rome, and I had a feeling that I was missing something.

Rome grunted. "It's not my fault that Tara moved in next to you. It's your fault for telling me that you had an opening."

"When I said that my renters moved out, I thought that you were going to move in, not your crazy ex," he explained.

Ah.

Rome's ex was a woman named Tara, and she had lived next to Liner for a time while her son was going through chemo treatments.

Rome's son, Matias, hadn't made it.

And some time in between Matias being diagnosed and Matias passing away, Tara had run away and never looked back.

That was all that I knew, and I knew better than to even touch on this subject by trying to find out more right now. I'd have to ask Wade later when there was no possibility that we'd be heard by Rome.

How About No

"I can tell you now that Debbie Doozy doesn't have any dogs. Hell, she only has her kids every other weekend, and I fuckin' cringe when that day comes around," Liner mumbled, squeezing his way into the circle between me and Bayou.

I leaned a little more heavily into Wade, who took my weight with ease despite the fact that his leg was still bothering him.

"What do you mean by cringing when the kids come?"

My protective instincts were raring, and if two little girls that I had held and loved on since they were tiny little babies were suffering, I wanted to know.

Liner's eyes turned down to study me.

"I think there's more yelling going on than there is parenting," Liner said. "I don't ever hear specifics, because she rarely comes outside with them except to put them in her van and to take them where they're meant to be going, but the muted screams through her closed doors, as well as the way she looks when I glance at her through the open front windows…yeah, I wouldn't want to be her kids."

I swallowed hard and felt my fist clench.

Then a wet nose briefly touched the back of my hand, and I looked down to see Capo close—but looking the other way.

My heart lightened a small amount.

"I need to get on my Facebook page and start doing damage control," I sighed. "Hopefully I don't have to pay back all those donors. I don't have the money to do that, but this whole situation makes me feel awful."

Wade's arm tightened around my waist briefly. "We'll figure it out, honey."

His low rumbled assurance had me believing him, even though I had a feeling it wasn't going to be that easy.

And I was right.

The moment that I posted about the woman on my dog rescue page, the shit hit the fan.

One, Debbie Schultz went nuclear and started a war by declaring us business partners and accusing me of stealing people's money—though I only knew that secondhand since I'd blocked ol' Debbie Doozy.

Two, people started to demand their money back—from me.

Three, someone tried to set my daycare on fire.

CHAPTER 15

I give just enough fucks to stay employed and out of the back of my husband's police cruiser.

-Landry's secret thoughts

Landry

"No," I moaned, looking at the firetrucks putting out the blaze that'd started in the storage shed beside the daycare.

"They have it contained, honey," Wade promised. "The building is perfectly fine. The only thing that we're going to have to worry about right now is the electric. But that was turned off when this all began."

"I'm not going to be able to open tomorrow," I murmured.

"No," he agreed. "Once they clear the building to us, I'll get an electrician out here to disconnect the power to the storage shed from the main breaker. when that's done, I'll get someone out here to remove the shed—after the insurance adjuster takes a look." He paused. "But, even when you can reopen, I don't think that you should—not until we get this crazy bitch squared away."

"Do you think the cameras caught anything?" I asked hopefully.

The state-of-the-art system had to come in handy at some point. All I'd really been able to utilize it for was firing employees who took naps during kids' nap times.

I'd appreciate it if something positive came out of this horrible day.

"I got the stuff." Liner came up to us, Hoax at his side.

Wade grunted. "Good. Take it to the house and see what you can find. Cameras twelve and fourteen have the best possibility of catching what we're looking for. But, hell, she might've done us a favor by being stupid and parked in the front lot."

I snorted. "She wouldn't be that dumb."

She *was* that dumb.

***

"I wasn't there!" a woman screamed at the top of her lungs. "I was at home in bed!"

I'd come into the police station get my restraining order against the woman currently screaming. When Wade and I had walked in, it was to see all hell breaking loose in the bullpen.

Why you ask?

Because Debbie didn't like being accused of something that "she didn't do" according to her.

Except we'd seen her do it. Mostly.

Her van had been parked in full view of the cameras that Wade had trained on the driveway, and there was no mistaking the letters on the license plates or the stickers on the back glass declaring her a member of the Bear Bottom PTA.

"All right, you're all set," Castiel said, handing me the paperwork. "Since she's here, we'll go ahead and inform her of her limitations when it comes to you. But, just sayin', she'll likely stay pretty far away after she was caught doing this."

Wade grunted. "I doubt it."

"Well, she didn't make bail because she spit on the judge," Castiel said, eyes twinkling. "And you know how ol' Judge Painter is. He doesn't tolerate this kind of behavior on the best of days."

I tuned them out.

I was tired.

I hadn't slept in well over twenty-four hours, and honestly, I was ready to go fucking home.

I was so tired that I couldn't even work up any rage over the fact that she was likely responsible for burning down mine and Wade's house. I was just happy that she'd been caught pretty much red-handed doing the same to my business.

My phone vibrated again, but I didn't pull it out of my pocket this time.

I knew that it was someone wanting their money back—money I didn't have to give.

But hopefully once this was all settled, I'd be able to file a civil suit against her that would generate the funds to repay all of the people who had so graciously donated.

"Let's go home, honey," Wade said, giving me a slight jiggle.

I blinked, unaware that I'd gone so far into my head.

"Okay," I said, bringing my eyes up only to find Castiel staring at me with confusion.

"What?"

He didn't say anything, only looked at me.

Not in the mood for his shit, either, I turned on my heel and started walking as fast as my rapidly deteriorating body could muster.

Wade caught up with me just as I passed the desk that Debbie was currently chained and cuffed to.

She saw me, and her eyes narrowed. "You bitch!"

I stopped, unwilling to allow this moment to pass.

"What did you do to the dogs that you stole?" I hissed.

Debbie's lips twitched. "Had them put to sleep. The humane thing to do."

I narrowed my eyes. "The dogs—the ones that I fight for—aren't on death's door. They're older and have at least a few more years of good times left in them. They are not ready to die."

Debbie scoffed. "Whatever. You don't need to be taking care of any dogs. You're pretty shitty at watching things that are important."

I didn't miss the underlying accusation.

"I'm sorry," I told her. "I've already told you I'm sorry a hundred times. But, Debbie? You not watching your daughter wasn't my fault. It was yours. I'm not sure why you can't see that."

With that, I left before I said something that I'd regret.

Wade stayed silent as well until we got home—to his home that had absolutely nothing in it still. The moment we got inside, he didn't let me get more than a foot in the direction of the bedroom before he stopped me with a hand on my wrist.

I turned and didn't stop moving until my face was buried in his chest.

"I just want it all to go away." I moaned.

He inched my shirt up and let his palms smooth over the skin of my lower back.

"We'll figure it out, baby," he promised. "And when you're done freaking out over this, we need to start looking at houses. We got our check from the insurance adjuster for it."

How About No

I blew out a breath. "They covered everything?"

"Yep," he promised. "Now all you need to do is find somewhere. Though, I was thinking if you were open to it, we might purchase some land and use the check to build the house."

That sounded...divine.

"I like that idea," I said sleepily, not realizing what exactly I was agreeing to—IE building a house with Wade, which smacked of permanence.

Then suddenly I was up in his arms.

Wrapping my arm around his neck, I tried to ignore the fact that he was limping heavily and not as steady on his feet as he used to be.

It was only when I jolted hard that I said, "Maybe you should put me down."

"Capo decided not to move out of the middle of the floor and I had to sidestep him and shifted you in my arms as I did," he explained. "I wasn't almost falling."

I snorted. "You don't know what I was thinking."

"I know you," he promised. "I also know that I want to lay you down in that bed and make you forget your day."

Which he did moments later.

Following me down once he placed me directly in the center, his mouth met mine, and I decided that sleep was overrated. Especially when you had a man like Wade in your bed willing to make you forget your bad day.

"Lift your hips," he instructed.

I did, and he yanked the comforter out from underneath of us, tossing it somewhere in the vicinity of the floor.

Before I could gasp or protest the fact that the blanket was now touching the ground, Wade's mouth came down on my neck. I hated when stuff fell on the floor. It seemed like it would be dirty to me after that happened, and I certainly didn't have time to be washing a comforter tonight.

He started to press soft, wet kisses down my throat, tracing a path to the neckline of my shirt.

"Shirt off," he urged.

He didn't help me except to push himself up on his arms, lifting his weight off of me from the waist up.

It was then I felt the hard column of his cock press into my most delicate place, and I smiled.

"What's the creepy smile for?" he teased.

I lifted my shirt up over my head, then stuck my tongue out at him before tossing the shirt into his face.

He caught it without hesitation and tossed it on the floor, likely near the comforter.

I snickered when he looked pointedly at the bra.

"You said shirt," I told him. "I specifically heard shirt."

He rolled his eyes and grunted at me. "Get it off."

I took it off but didn't throw it at him. Instead, I rolled slightly—as much as his body on mine would allow—and tossed the bra on the nightstand for me to put back on tomorrow.

I was still down to limited clothing choices, and if this hit the floor, I'd have to wash it. I was anal, so sue me.

Wade's hand smoothed down the exposed expanse of my back and stopped at the curve of my ass to give it a little squeeze. "Pants, too."

I rolled my eyes but went ahead and completely disrobed before flopping back onto the bed. "Better?"

His eyes went down the length of my body, stopping to linger at my breasts and the apex of my thighs. "Much."

Then he dropped down and pressed his mouth to mine and totally destroyed my bad mood with one single kiss.

Thoroughly.

"God, your mouth is intoxicating," he growled, dragging his bearded face down the length of my jaw. "All day I wanted to pull you in tight and keep everything and everyone away from you. But you wouldn't have allowed me to do that, would you?"

Hell no.

He knew better than that.

I wasn't the type of woman to be coddled, and it warmed my heart that he realized that.

He knew me better than I knew myself.

"No," I breathed, feeling my stomach clench when he hit that spot just below my ear with the tip of his tongue. "I would've hated it."

He growled against my skin. "It's not a bad thing to allow someone to take care of you," he teased, running his hand up the length of one thigh.

His callused hand felt rough and unforgiving against the smooth skin and I thanked my earlier judgment of shaving my legs with Wade's razor as I moved to capture the mouth I loved so much.

"So fuckin' smooth," he whispered, echoing my earlier thoughts.

"I like your razor," I told him. "You might need to go get me one exactly like it."

He pulled back so he could see my face. "You shaved your legs with my razor?"

I nodded. "I also shaved my bikini line," I felt it prudent to point out.

He snorted. "I thought we had that talk before when we were married. You are not, under any circumstance, allowed to use my razor on your pubic hair."

I rolled my eyes. "I remember you saying earlier that you missed having all of my shit lying around. Even missed all the weird things that I used to do."

He had said that, almost verbatim, while we were getting ready to go file my protection order.

He'd said he missed all my stray hairs that I left on the counter after brushing my hair and the way that I never managed to put the lid on the toothpaste or my deodorant. Then there was the fact that I hung my bras up in the shower, forcing him to move them almost daily before he took his morning shower after his workout.

"I also don't remember mentioning that I liked shaving my neck and plucking your pubes out of my mouth." He paused. "Any other time, like when I go down on you, is perfectly fine. But when I'm shaving? Yeah, I don't like that."

I lifted my hand and let it rest against his neck. "How do you possibly get my pubes into your mouth when you're only shaving your neck?"

He shrugged, hitting me with that grin that never ceased in making my heart race.

"It's kind of like asking how the fuck your hair finds its way into my ass crack." He paused. "I can guarantee your hair wasn't anywhere near there."

I felt a grin start to overtake my face. "I was there the day before yesterday," I pointed out. "Remember, I was massaging your back?"

He rolled his eyes. "I had underwear on when you were doing that."

True.

"I also found it after I took a shower."

I shrugged.

"That's just one of life's unexplainable phenomena, then," I teased.

He pushed my leg up and out to the side, making my lower half become almost completely open to his gaze.

The cool air on my overheated pussy felt damn near unbearable.

His eyes lifted to mine. "Unzip me."

I went a step further and unbuttoned him, as well as pushed his pants down his hips while I was at it.

He didn't object to my attentions until I reached out to wrap my hand around his distended cock.

"Don't," he said when my fingertips brushed his cock head. "I want you to put your hands above your head."

I blinked, staring at him in stunned silence. "Why?"

He'd never denied me before, and his refusal to allow me to touch him honestly shocked the hell out of me.

"Because I want to do things to your body, and to do that, I need to hold on to at least a little bit of my control," he explained. "I can't do that when your hand is touching me."

Slightly mollified, I reached my hands up above my head and grabbed the bottom of the wooden headboard.

His eyes drank me in while I did what he asked. "Why does that give you such a sense of satisfaction?" I questioned.

"You're doing exactly what I asked you to do," he stated, pushing up so that his cock now lay against the exposed center of me. "Now why would that be a turn on?"

I rolled my eyes. "You're terrible."

He ground himself down onto me. "Maybe. Maybe not. Whatever the reason for it, I don't care. Pull your other leg up and out like this one."

He gave the one he still had in his grasp a squeeze, and I felt things inside of me clench.

I loved it when he was in charge and acting like this.

I shifted my weight and actually bumped against his hurt leg, causing him to flinch. "God, Wade. I'm sorry."

He leaned down and pressed a kiss against my downturned mouth. "Didn't hurt that bad. Honestly, just a surprise."

I scowled, causing him to laugh. "Really. I swear it didn't hurt that bad."

I instinctively started to reach for him with the hand that wasn't holding up my leg where he wanted it, and he shook his head. "Nuh-uh. Put that one back up on the headboard."

I did as he asked, putting it up on the top rail while also digging my nails into the back of my thigh where my hand rested, holding my leg in place.

I felt exposed and raw, and I wasn't sure where he was going with this whole thing.

"On second thought," he said, gesturing to my leg with his head. "You take this leg, too."

I did, hooking both arms around the backs of my knees and pulling them even farther up and out.

The moment that I was where he wanted me, he started to rock his hips.

The tail end of his shirt tickled my belly, and I wanted nothing more than to fist it and yank it off of his body.

"What do you want?"

He'd always been able to read me so easily, sometimes I was surprised by how well he was able to tell when something was bothering me.

"I want you to take your shirt off," I growled.

In fact, I wanted nothing more than to feel the hair covering his groin drag against my clit.

Which he easily interpreted with only a small grimace on my part.

He ripped the shirt off and over his head by hooking his thumb into the collar at the base of his neck and yanking it up and off of his head.

I wasn't sure why it was always so sexy to see a man—my man—take off his shirt, but goddamn was it a sight to see.

Wade had never been what you'd call a tidy man. He was a very hairy guy, and his chest was one of the places that I loved to drag my fingers along while absently reading a book. He had a chest full of hair, and his lower happy trail connected up the center of his abs to the chest hair that grew in copiously.

It was dark brown, matching the color of his beard, and made his chest appear even bigger than it actually was.

But his man pelt as I'd so kindly named it when we were first married was one of my favorite features about the man.

My eyes likely dilated at the sight before me, and Wade started to chuckle as he caught the move.

"I don't understand what your fascination is," he teased me. "But I fucking like it."

"It's like why I'll never understand your fascination with my boobs," I pointed out. "We'll just have to realize that there are things in this world that can't be explained."

He scoffed. "More like you're just weird," he pointed out. "It's fairly normal for men to be turned on by breasts."

"And it's fairly normal for a woman to find a hairy chest attractive," I countered.

Just as the last words came out of my mouth, Wade bent down and captured one distended nipple into his mouth and sucked.

My pussy clenched on empty air, and I felt downright bereft without something inside of me to clench on to.

Something he must've sensed by again reading my face because his grin went wider as he reached down and plunged two fingers into my wetness.

My eyes slammed shut, and my nails dug in deeper.

"Jesus," I hissed, back arching.

All it took was two pumps of his fingers for me to realize that I was so not liking this no touching him thing. I wanted to wrap my legs around his hips. I really wanted to pull him down on top of me and latch my teeth into his shoulder muscle as he took me hard.

And I *reallllly* wanted to come.

"Don't tease me, Wade," I pleaded. "Either take me or make me come. Please."

Wade curled his fingers, and I knew right then and there that he'd liked the pleading, and had decided to give me what I wanted.

"Oh, God," I breathed, feeling him stroke that secret, special spot inside of me that I'd never been able to find on my own.

Yet, without so much as a question, Wade always seemed to find it with little to no effort.

Then again, it could be like me when I went down on him. It was easy to remember the things that pleased my man, and it didn't matter that years had passed since I'd done some of them. It was like the things that made Wade weak in the knees were always burned into my memory.

I knew that he liked it when I flicked that little spot on the underside of his cock. I also knew that he liked his balls to be squeezed just this side of too hard when I was giving him a hand job.

And just like that, Wade made me come.

Hard.

I screamed through clenched teeth, unable to find it in me to open my eyes. I desperately wanted to, though. I loved seeing the satisfaction in Wade's eyes as he made me come. It'd always been one of those things that only served to turn me on more.

Breathing hard, I finally felt my back drop back to the bed and opened my eyes.

Wade was staring at me, one hand still frozen inside of me while the other was wrapped around his cock as he slowly pumped away at it, getting off on the sight of me getting off.

Feeling an aching in my legs, I let them drop to the bed and released them, then held my hands out in a silent plea for my man to come to me.

He came willingly, letting go of his cock in the process.

He growled when his mouth came down on mine. "You're so fuckin' beautiful when you come."

I felt heat rising to my face, and I turned my mouth so that my lips rested against the fast beat of his pulse.

"You make me feel beautiful," I breathed.

He situated himself between my splayed legs, then suddenly rolled so that we were on our sides.

There, he made long, sweet love to me.

His thrusts were slow and deep, driving me wild all while being sweet about it.

His hands never loosened around me, even when our sweat started to make us slip and slide.

And when I finally came for the second time, he did, too.

Deep inside of me where he belonged and always would.

Once our breathing was back to normal, and his cock was once again flaccid and resting against the inside of my thigh, I told him my deepest sorrow.

"I made a very bad decision," I told Wade. "I was scared. So freakin' mad at you I couldn't think. And honestly, I hated that you were so sympathetic to my sister when you never even asked me how my childhood affected me." I paused. "I hate it that you still talk to her. I hate it even more that my parents acted like I was their golden child just to get you onboard for the surgery when it couldn't be further from the truth."

"Your parents are good," he said, sounding sick to his stomach. "They made it sound like you'd only donated once. Had I known it was as many as it was, I would've..."

"Done the same thing, because you're a big ol' softy," I countered.

He groaned into my shoulder. "I would take every single thing back if I could. God, I'm sorry. I'm so sorry."

I wrapped my arms around his head and squeezed it tight.

He made a protesting sound into my armpit. "Staaaaap."

I snickered and squeezed harder.

His hands came up, and all of a sudden, I was no longer the one in charge, he was.

And I was on the bottom, his legs on either side of my ribs, while he tickled the crap out of me.

"Wade!" I cried out loudly. "Noooo!"

By the time he stopped, I was crying from laughing so hard, and I barely caught my breath before he was switching gears back to where we'd previously been only ten minutes before.

With this new position he was in, his balls were resting on my chest, and his large cock was growing bigger by the second, bisecting my breasts.

His eyes were now heated, and he was staring at me like I was about to really like what he was about to do to me.

"How can you already be hard?" I questioned, voice barely over a whisper.

His eyes went from my breasts to my eyes. "Do you see where I'm sitting right now?"

I looked down, opened my mouth to reply that I did, in fact, see where he was sitting, and he took advantage of my position and pushed his cock into my mouth.

I teasingly bit down, and his eyes flared.

Then we did it all over again. This time hard and fast, but still just as sweet.

Lani Lynn Vale

CHAPTER 16

Apparently, the correct response to 'see you later, alligator' is not 'after supper, motherfucker.'

Who knew?

-Wade to Landry

Wade

"I'm gonna be somebody, someday!" my wife—my very drunk wife—sang loudly with the song that was playing through the speakers.

Bayou's eyes met mine and promptly slid away. "You know, I'm actually kind of impressed how well she holds a tune."

I chuckled. "She sings pretty damn good when she's not drunk. It doesn't surprise me that she sings well when she is...although at this point I'm really quite surprised she's hitting all the notes. She's on beer seven, I think..."

"Eight," Izzy replied, mirth filling her eyes. "I think she finished her eighth as she was walking toward the food table. That's her bottle that Linc is holding."

We all looked over to where Linc and his wife were standing. Conleigh and Landry were now slow dancing to a very fast-paced song while Linc watched on, extremely amused.

"I think she got sidetracked," I admitted, finding it amusing that my wife had let her hair down and had actually had some fun after the day that she'd had.

"I really like her," Izzy murmured, watching as Linc walked toward us with delight written all over his face. "She's the sweetest person I've ever met. Did you know that she said I could drop off the baby at her daycare whenever I needed to?"

I felt my heart pang at that.

"She wants a baby," I murmured, watching Landry stumble and right herself.

She looked down at the offending object that'd tripped her—her own feet—and scowled.

Moments later, her heels were kicked off in the direction of our table and she was once again dancing, though now Conleigh and Landry had switched to line dancing.

"Then give her one," Linc said as he caught the tail end of our conversation.

I felt things inside of me clench.

"If I could, I would," I murmured. "But, when Landry was a teenager, she had an infection that got out of control and they had to remove her ovaries and fallopian tubes."

Izzy blew out a breath. "Shit. That makes me feel awful."

It did me, too.

Every single day since we'd found out that we were still married and that I wasn't going to let her go again, I'd been thinking about ways to make this better. To give her the things that we both wanted.

And I'd finally decided that adoption was likely the way to go.

Only, I had no clue whatsoever where to start.

"When she told me that she wanted to start the daycare when we first met, I had no clue why. She said she loved kids, and that she'd always wanted to do it." I paused, unsure if I should go on, but at a loss for how to handle the situation without putting my ass in the fire again—so to speak. "She wants kids. She wants them badly. The only problem is that she can't have them and that I can...she said she always wanted to have a baby that looks like me, with my hair. I'm not sure if that means that I should offer to find a surrogate and we use my stuff, or we straight up go for adoption. I'm so fuckin' scared of losin' her that I don't want to say anything wrong and risk offending her."

There was silence for a few long seconds, making me fear the worst.

"She won't leave you again," Bayou finally spoke up. "I think she was just as broken up about everything as you were, to be honest."

My eyes turned to the man who at one time had supported my decision to leave Landry be.

"Why'd you tell me to leave her alone?" I asked carefully.

Bayou didn't look the least bit apologetic. "It's hard for someone to know what they're missing if they're reminded every single day of why they should stay apart."

I frowned. "What?"

"She was so fuckin' pissed at you that she couldn't see past the pain," Bayou continued. "Whatever you did to her hurt her. Bad. And she needed to get rid of that pain that you caused her before she could see past it. You gave her the time to do that, and when the opportunity arose for her to rethink her choices, she finally saw past it and looked at you. She missed you and was no longer blinded by what you'd done. By doing that, she chose you rationally, instead of choosing you irrationally."

"Irrationally?" Rome asked. "Bayou, you're speaking in goddamn riddles."

"I understand." Zee startled me by entering into the conversation. "My ex-wife? I pissed her off good by joining the military straight out of high school. We'd just gotten married, had a baby on the way, and I couldn't see past my fear of not being able to support our family. So, I went and joined. She was justifiably pissed because we didn't get to make that decision together, and while I was gone at basic, she mostly got over being that pissed. Until she miscarried at fifteen weeks without me there. When I got done at basic, she met me at graduation only to have me sign divorce papers. All I'm saying is that time really does heal all wounds…it can also cause more. In Landry's case, y'all needed more time. I think that's what Bayou is trying to say. That's why you didn't go barging in there and demanding that she come back the moment that you realized you'd made a huge mistake."

I looked at the ground and thought about his words, then took a deep breath and told them what I'd done that had hurt Landry so much.

"Matias had a donor match in an eighteen-year-old," Rome murmured, sounding sad. "His little brother had also been a recipient of his bone marrow when he was sixteen. It's hard, according to that kid. And I'll forever be grateful for what that kid did for Matias. But, on the other hand, I would never have allowed him to give my son that much. Plus, knowing that she was just a kid while this happened? They were supposed to protect her and didn't. I can see how you choosing to help the sister would bring up bad memories for her."

I looked down at my feet and cursed. "I know that. *Now*."

Rome grinned then and pulled his wife close. "Just don't fuck up anymore. Always choose her. I think you won't have any problems keeping her."

"What makes you think that?" I looked at the bigger man.

Rome tilted his head at something at my back, and I turned to find Landry still dancing, only this time it was with her eyes directly on me.

"Because someone who hasn't taken her eyes off of you all night long, even with all this man candy all around her, obviously sees something in you that she doesn't want to lose," Izzy pointed out.

I felt my lips twitch.

"And she makes you less grumpy. So, you'll want to hold onto her," Izzy continued.

I rolled my eyes. "I'm sure getting shot had nothing to do with that grumpiness."

"You were a grumpy bastard well before you were shot, and we all know it," Linc offered.

I sighed and shrugged. "It's just me, what can I say?"

"Who's ready for dinner?" Conleigh yelled.

We turned once again to see Landry wobbling and Conleigh attempting to guide their way to us with over eight pizza boxes a piece. Conleigh had the boxes she was carrying resting on her baby bump while one hand was holding Landry's elbow.

Both Linc and I immediately started forward. "Who the hell thought it was a good idea to give the food to the drunk girl and her pregnant friend?"

"This girl has cash," Landry informed me as soon as she was close enough. "And apparently the pizza guy doesn't care whether I'm drunk or not as long as I gave him a tip."

Chuckling, I took the pizza boxes from Conleigh's grasp and walked them over to the bar, unsurprised when I felt Landry leaning up against me as she started to peek into the boxes. "Where's the one with the pineapple on it?"

A few of the guys made a gagging sound.

"Oh, I love pineapple!" Conleigh cheered.

"No, you don't," Linc countered. "You don't like pineapple, just like you don't like peppers."

"Well, I like the smell of pineapples." She paused. "I also like the way they're so pretty. I have some sparkly flip-flops with them on it. You want to borrow them sometime, Landry?"

Landry's eyes went sad for a few seconds. "I don't have any more flip-flops. I only have the tennis shoes that I'm wearing. Did you know that my house burned down with all my stuff inside of it?"

I felt a pang in my chest.

We'd been so busy over the last few days that we hadn't even had a chance to go check the house—or what remained of it.

That was on our plan for tomorrow, actually. Or had been.

Honestly, that was the last straw for Landry after the day she'd had, and instead of doing the whole adult thing, she decided to get drunk instead of facing her responsibilities.

But again, it'd all be there tomorrow. Today, she was allowed to unwind.

"Seems like you may need to get your husband to take you shopping," Conleigh gasped. "Oh! I can take you shopping!"

Linc groaned at the same time I did.

My leg was feeling better, sure, but goddamn. There was no way I was up to walking for miles and miles on end while the damn woman decided to try on every single outfit that may or may not look good on her.

Honestly, that was the one thing about being married that I did not miss—going shopping.

Landry tried every single thing within a ten-mile radius that was her size. Whether she needed a formal dress or not, it was going on.

"I don't want to go," Linc whined.

"I'll give you my credit card and you can shop online," I offered hopefully.

Landry turned, a half-finished slice of pizza in her hand, and frowned. "Are you trying to tell me that you wouldn't go with me so I can have some new clothes?"

I paused, unsure how to answer this.

"I don't think I can go with you," I told her, playing up my disability to get out of mall shopping. "I may be able to walk a little bit, but you know how constant standing hurts my leg. I could do maybe an hour, tops."

Landry sniffed. "I don't need you there. I have a car."

She did.

And Debbie was in jail so…

"Okay," I said. "But if you need me, you'll call."

Landry took another bite of her pizza. "I'll call."

"I'm going!" Conleigh twisted the top off another beer and handed it to Landry. "And we're gonna have to go tomorrow. I need new underwear."

Linc sighed.

"Why do you need more underwear, Conleigh?" Izzy laughed.

Before she could answer, Linc put his hand over his wife's mouth. "Let's not talk about this right now, okay?"

Chuckles sounded around the bar that they'd all gathered around to start eating, and I chose a piece of pizza that most certainly did not have pineapples on it.

After practically inhaling it, I groaned.

"God, that was good." I sighed. "Did they deliver my salad?"

"I told them to take the salad off," Landry said around a mouthful of crust. "Nobody wants a salad from there. Eat the pizza."

"Landry," I growled.

"Pizza's not going to kill you." Landry narrowed her eyes. "Unless you think I'm fat?"

Chuckles sounded again, and this time I was not one to join them.

"No," I told her honestly. "I don't think you're fat."

Where the fuck did that come from?

"Then you should have no problem eating pizza, because you're in better shape than I am," she countered. "Make me happy and eat some of those Cinnastix, too. Jesus, this pineapple is good."

Rolling my eyes, I reached for another piece.

"Your convoluted explanation makes no sense," I told her as I reached for another beer.

"Whatever." She rolled her eyes. "You're eating the pizza, and that's all that matters."

If she said so.

***

Two hours later, it was just after midnight, and I smelled smoke.

Following the scent with a wary expression on my face, I came to a sudden halt when I got a load of what my wife was doing.

I looked up to see Landry holding a paper that was burning. Fire licked up the sides of it and climbed into the air, and ashes were falling to the ground by her feet.

I blinked and walked toward her, gently taking the burning paper from her hands and tossing it into the bathroom sink where it finished burning.

It was only after I studied the paper for a few long seconds that I saw *what* she was burning.

"Ummm," I hesitated, looking over at her. "Why'd you burn our divorce decree?"

Her eyes were hazy as she blinked. "So, you can't return me."

That's when I threw my head back and laughed, walking forward so that I could wrap my arms around her waist.

"Who says I'd ever return you?" I questioned.

She bit her lip and looked down.

I caught her chin and forced her to look back up. "Baby?"

"I'm so bad at this thing, Wade," she whispered. "I'm always screwing up. I'm always emotional. I'm just…fucked up. I'm wishy-washy, and not a day goes by that I wish I hadn't done the things I'd done to us. And you treat me like I'm the beginning and the end of your world. Why do you deal with my shit?"

I bent forward and dropped my mouth down on hers.

"Why do you deal with mine?" I asked. "This last month? It's been awful. I've been on bitch duty while my leg healed at the rate of a goddamn slug, and I've been in a god-awful mood. Yet, each day you make time to make me feel important. You've taken me to work with you. You don't complain when I go with you everywhere and walk slow—holding you back. You have lunch with me before going to the rescue…and you act like I'm not fucked up, too. I love you."

She rolled her eyes. "Wade, unlike you, I don't see anything wrong with you. Not one single thing."

I rolled my eyes. "So, you're telling me that having me follow you around day in and day out doesn't bother you?"

Because I had done that. I'd followed her around, from room to room, almost as if she was leaving me at any second. As if what we had was something that might disappear if I didn't keep an eye on it.

"Actually," she said softly. "That's been my favorite part of having you back. You being there when I wake up from a nap. Me coming out of the dog kennels after cleaning shit up for an hour. Wade, why do you think I haven't freaked out that our house burned down and all of my stuff inside of it was ruined?"

I gave her a look that clearly said that she had, indeed, freaked out.

Landry waved it away. "I'm a little freaked out, sure. I'm pissed off at the situation, yes. But, did you ever stop to think that I'm taking this incredibly well?"

Yes, I had.

"Yes," I replied hesitantly. "But I just assumed it was because nothing super important was lost in the fire. It was only material things, and honestly, that house held some bad memories for me and you. I just assumed your feelings and mine were the same on the matter."

Her eyes went wide. "You had bad feelings about the house?"

I snorted. "You lived in it with another man while we were supposedly divorced. Of course, I had some ill-will regarding it."

Her eyes went soft. "Kourt asked me today if we were going to renew our vows."

My eyes sharpened. "Do you want to?"

She looked at the still smoldering ashes in the sink. "I want to get married again. I want to do it all over again. I want it to feel real."

I took a step in her direction and hooked an arm around her waist, pulling her to me. "You're saying that what we have doesn't feel real?"

She shook her head with frustration plainly written on her face. "I'm saying that I fucked things up, and I want to make sure that you remember you're mine. I want everyone to know that you're mine."

I looked down at her hand—which still didn't have my wedding ring back on it.

"Where's your ring?" I asked.

I didn't bother to ponder it being lost in the fire. I'd seen the box in her purse last week when I went through her bottomless pit in search of ibuprofen. I'd seen it in the middle section, all by itself, as if it was just taunting me to put it back on her hand.

"My purse on the counter," she whispered.

I didn't waste a second going to retrieve it.

Stepping over Capo who was laying peacefully in the middle of the kitchen, I winced only slightly at the jarring movement before quickly retrieving her ring and walking back to our bathroom.

Once I was back in front of her, I opened the box and stared at the ring.

"This ring means you're mine," I told her, not taking my eyes off of the piece of diamond and metal that had changed my life the moment I'd slipped it onto her finger.

"I was yours whether I had that ring on or not," she whispered. "I've been yours since the moment that I walked into your classroom."

I felt my heart swell as I reached for her hand.

"I'll marry you again," I told her. "I'll pay for another ten-thousand-dollar wedding if it makes you smile at me like I've lit your entire world."

Sliding the ring on her finger, I felt something inside of me once again become whole at the sight.

Her breath caught, and I finally lifted my gaze back to hers.

Her eyes were blazing with the same emotion that was filling my own chest—euphoria.

"Where's yours?" She licked her lips.

I reached into my pocket and pulled it out.

A day hadn't passed that I hadn't had it with me.

The day that I almost died next to my car, I'd slipped it onto my finger while I'd been laying in my own pool of blood.

Her cool, delicate fingers brushed mine as she reached for the solid hunk of gold. It was scratched and no longer as polished as it'd once been, but it didn't matter. That piece of metal resembled us—solid and strong despite all the damage that it'd been put through.

She reached for my hand, and I snickered. "Other hand, baby."

"Oh," she rolled her eyes, swaying slightly on her feet. "Yeah, I knew that."

She'd done the same thing at our wedding—reached for the wrong hand. I teased her about it constantly over the course of our marriage, so it only seemed fitting that she'd do it now, too.

Clumsily she slipped the metal onto my finger and made a frustrated face when it wouldn't go past my second knuckle. "Give it a twist, baby."

She did, and the ring finally slipped fully on, sliding into place exactly where it was always meant to be.

"I'm never, not ever, going to let go again. I promise, Wade."

Her shining eyes, and her perfect mouth saying those words were exactly what my heart needed to hear.

"Good," I told her firmly. "Because I would've followed you wherever you went."

Her smile was brilliant. "Now, take me to bed. I feel like I'm about to topple over."

I took her to bed, then I made love to her until she passed out from my attentions.

All the while I wondered if life was too good to be true.

CHAPTER 17

Why is it called boob sweat? Why not humidititties?

-One of life's unanswered questions

Wade

All the good mood from the night—or early morning—before was now gone.

With both of us standing on the front lawn that we had seeded with our own two hands, it was hard to see anything in this situation at all positive.

Not with the grass a black blob, nor with the tree we'd planted the day we moved in charred to a barely distinguishable cinder.

Hell, even the mailbox hadn't been spared, and that, I remembered, had been an arm and a leg to build because Landry had wanted a fuckin' dolphin of all things.

"This is bad," she said softly. "I don't think there's a single thing that we can salvage."

I didn't think so either.

"Even the lawn furniture is gone," she whispered. "My mailbox, the one that I loved—gone. The stupid gnome is even broken."

The gnome was what finally broke her heart.

"Awww, baby." I curled my arm around her shoulders and dropped a kiss onto her head. "It'll be okay."

"I don't see how," she sniffled. "It's gone. Not even our weeping willow survived."

I dropped one more kiss onto her head and let her go, my eyes on the outside.

The inside was a total loss. The only thing left standing were the outside walls, and even those were well on their way to falling down thanks to the support beams being charred to cinder at the foundation.

Unluckily for us, there'd been a second house fire that had started about an hour before ours had, and the entire volunteer fire department had been at that one trying to keep it from spreading to neighboring homes. Our house had burned to the ground, and not a single drop of water had hit it until two hours after it'd started.

Though, that likely had more to do with the fact that the other home that'd been on fire was one that was threatening other neighbors while ours had been at the end of a block.

"Did they give you what you put into it?"

I turned to see the county arson investigator's assistant, better known as Castiel, standing behind me.

Castiel was a jack of all trades just like Zee was, and had started the arson investigating about two years ago when the old fire marshal had lost his right-hand man. Castiel had stepped in for a few weeks to cover for him. That few weeks had turned into a few months, and those few months had turned into two years.

Castiel still said that he was planning on moving on from the job, but he hadn't done it yet.

"They gave me what I wanted," I told him bluntly. "It didn't cover the furnishings or all the decking outside in the backyard, but that's to be expected. Luckily, Landry was safe. That's all I really care about."

Castiel was quiet a moment. "I feel like a dick for being so mean to her since y'all separated."

I cast him a sideways glance. "She understands. It's hard to be faced with the choice of choosing your good friend over the woman you met because of the friend."

"Still," he grunted. "I'm not proud of the way I acted."

"But you're human," Landry's soft voice said from behind us. "And we all make mistakes, even though I am happy that you stayed loyal to Wade. He deserved that, not me."

But Cass and I both turned to survey the woman looking so heartbroken standing behind us.

I kept my mouth shut, realizing that this was something that Castiel and Landry needed to discuss, or it'd never get straightened out.

A lot of the guys were likely feeling much the same way, but none of them had been as vocal about their dislike of each other more than Landry and Castiel.

Castiel was one of my best friends, and even though we didn't have much time to hang out due to our jobs and our obligations, we still knew that we each had the other's back.

"You deserved to be treated differently than the way I treated you," he murmured. "Suffice it to say, I should've been able to control my anger, but that has nothing to do with you, and everything to do with the fact that the same thing happened to me. But where you both have a happy ending—I didn't."

"I never knew you were married," Landry said softly.

Castiel looked up at the burnt remains of our house. "A lot of years ago I met someone who I thought loved me like I loved her. I was wrong, and she showed me that by packing up and left to pursue her dream of acting."

Landry cleared her throat. "That's tough. And I hope one day to hear the entire story."

Castiel grinned, but before he could say anything else, a white semi-lifted newer model Chevy Silverado pulled up to the curb and Conleigh hopped out.

She looked tired, but her welcoming smile instantly put a smile on Landry's face.

Linc, who'd stayed over by the truck with his phone at his ear, started to argue with someone on the other end.

Conleigh ignored it and left him.

"Hey!" She practically skipped over, her feet faltering when she saw the melted gnome in the middle of the yard. "He's actually still kind of cute. You should keep him."

I looked down at the gnome. He was black with soot, half of him was melted, but he did still somewhat resemble what he was supposed to be.

Then Landry was bending down in front of me to pick him up, and I got a really good view of her cute little ass.

"I was thinking the same thing," she replied sadly.

"What are you doing here, Conleigh?" Castiel asked conversationally.

Conleigh's eyes went from the gnome to Cass. "I'm here to take Landry shopping."

"We're here to take Landry shopping," Linc groaned at the same time.

Cass made a gagging sound. "Have fun with that."

Conleigh and Landry giggled at his words and at the look of apparent disgust on Linc's face.

"Where, exactly, will y'all be going, and when will you be back?" I asked, then turned to Landry. "Remember that we have an appointment with the realtor this evening at seven."

I'd found a house while searching for land that was in my price range that I wanted Landry to take a look at. I had a feeling that she'd really like it.

"I'm going to take her to the mall," Conleigh informed me. "I'll have her back by dinner time."

I looked over at her husband and said, "She's going to have her back on time, isn't she?"

Linc snorted. "Conleigh talks a good game, but I can guarantee you that she's going to be tired in two hours tops. She'll have her back in time."

I looked over at Landry and thought much the same thing.

She went into work this morning at six after only getting three and a half hours of sleep—gotta love unreliable employees—then went straight from the daycare to the rescue, and she hadn't had time for a nap.

Hell, I could use one and I was used to the long hours with little sleep thanks to my job.

Landry looked like shit warmed over, but she seemed to get a little more pep back in her step at the thought of buying clothes.

"I'll get them back in time," Linc promised.

After offering him my hand, I pulled Landry in for a deep kiss.

"Be careful, baby. And have fun."

She rolled her eyes and smiled up at me. "I'm a cop's wife. We're always careful."

***

Landry

"You promised you wouldn't leave me again," he rasped against my skin.

I opened my eyes, brain completely confused, and tried to figure out where I was.

"Baby, please wake up."

I frowned, or tried to.

Something was over my mouth and nose. The air blowing at me was causing my mouth to hang open.

"Baby, please."

I took a deep breath and realized there was something wrong with my lungs. Something hurt. Something hurt very bad, and I couldn't figure out what it was.

I moaned, causing the weight that was resting on my forearm to jerk up in surprise.

That was when I realized that my eyes weren't quite as open as I'd thought they were. I could barely even see a tiny sliver of Wade's horrified face.

"Landry," he breathed, standing up. "Are you hurting? Do you know where you are?"

No.

I had no idea what was going on, or where I was.

Hell, I couldn't even get my eyes to open up all the way!

Whatever was over my mouth was making it difficult to speak, and I absently tried to reach for whatever it was and pull it off.

"Sir, I'm not going to ask you again to stay out of our way. If I have to repeat myself, you'll be removed from the ER," someone, a highly pissed off woman, said.

"Listen, girl," I heard said. Hoax. "I know that you're thinking you're helping, but you're not. You know how she was acting when she was brought in. The only way she calmed down was when he had her hand. Trust me when I say you need him."

"I agree that he helped her calm down," the woman sounded young. Not old. "But I can also achieve those same desired effects by using drugs. And, since y'all for some reason think it's better that she be awake so she can tell you what you think you need to know right now, I'm allowing that to happen. But I'm trying to work here. She's losing blood. I cannot have her getting harmed even worse because y'all won't stay out of my way."

I turned and tried to see the woman, which caused the mask that was covering my nose and mouth to dislodge slightly, allowing me to get a breath without having it forced straight down my throat.

The woman speaking to Hoax was a nurse.

She had a headful of blonde, curly hair. She was staring at Hoax like he was a pain in her ass, and I realized that I'd seen her somewhere before, but I couldn't place where.

"We'll behave, Pru," I heard Bayou say. "But don't make him leave."

My lips twitched.

That was where I knew her. She was Bayou's neighbor. The one who sat out on her porch a lot and watched the things happening around her without saying a word.

I liked her.

"Is she awake?"

That shrieked question came from someone on the other side of the curtain, beyond Bayou's neighbor.

Then the blue curtain was yanked back and Linc stood there, holding onto Conleigh's wheelchair like his life depended on it.

Conleigh had a cut above her eye, and her face was a mask of fatigue and horror.

"Yes," Wade said, retaking his seat. "She is. Baby, are you in pain?"

My eyes flicked back to those perfect ones that had always made me feel like my world was okay, and I smiled. "I'm okay."

That was a lie, of course.

There was something wrong with my stomach that felt like white-hot fire was roaring through it. That, and I couldn't feel my legs.

"You're such a bad liar, Landry." Wade smiled. "Ma'am," he turned to Pru. "She's in pain."

The nurse, who was doing something on the big computer by my feet, instantly went into action.

"I'll go tell the doctor," she said, turning on her heels.

I frowned. "Why?"

He didn't pretend not to understand me.

"Why are you here?" he asked.

I nodded, and pushed the mask farther away from my face, causing him to frown. "You need that on."

I shook my head and slapped feebly at his hand. "No. It makes my nose hurt."

The nurse was back, pulling the mask up to cover my mouth but not my nose. It didn't feel right, but it was better than having it where it had been. "It dries your nasal passages out. The doctor said I could get you started on a morphine pump."

I frowned.

Morphine?

I didn't know much about morphine, but what I did know was that it was used when a person was hurt and in a lot of pain.

"Why?" I repeated, turning my head back to Wade.

"You were shot," he said without preamble, shocking the absolute hell out of me. "Do you remember?"

Did I remember being shot? No.

Should that be something someone forgot about? I didn't think so.

"No." I shook my head at the same time as I said it. The mask that was covering my mouth made it hard for me to be heard, but Wade obviously understood it no problem.

"You were shot by a woman—she was outside the mall in a car with another woman. They sped away afterward," he continued.

My mouth fell open. "Someone shot me?"

He nodded, his face going hard. "The lady that shot you was apparently waiting for you to come out of the mall. She got you once in the stomach."

I blinked, completely dumbfounded that I would forget something so important as being shot.

"Wow," I finally settled on. "That's unfortunate."

Hoax snorted. "Unfortunate."

I wrinkled my nose at him. "You have a crush on the pretty nurse."

Said pretty nurse snorted. "He can't decide whether he wants to strangle me or kiss me. There's a line there between the two that he hasn't crossed over. My guess is at this point he wants to strangle me."

Yeah, right.

They looked like they wanted to tear each other's clothes off.

Especially with the way they were both glaring at each other. It was almost as if it'd been happening for a while now.

"Y'all are so going to have sex," I croaked.

Wade dropped his head to my arm and started to laugh.

Or cry.

With his face covered, I really couldn't tell mostly because both reactions caused his back to move in very similar ways.

Or at least, the way a person's back moved. I'd never actually seen Wade cry, so I really couldn't compare it to him crying because I'd never witnessed it before.

Both Hoax and Pru, the cute nurse, looked at me over Wade's shaking back.

They looked like I'd thrust my fist into their stomachs.

"What?" I said a little louder this time.

I honestly hadn't meant for them to hear me.

Or maybe I had. I wasn't too sure at this point.

My head was getting fuzzy again and I was finding it hard to keep my eyes open.

"Landry," someone said from beside me. "Look over here, sweetheart."

I frowned and did, finding Castiel standing there.

"You look like an angel of death," I informed him, biting my lip after I said it because I didn't want him to be mad at me. "I'm really sorry I hurt Wade. I didn't mean to. I only meant to make him realize that I was more importanter than my sister."

"Importanter's not a word, and I honestly understand now," he promised. "Do you remember what happened to you?"

I frowned. "I remember it felt like my soul had left my body when Wade went out there and hugged my sister. And when she started to cry as she tried to get her point across that I needed to donate, I broke a little bit inside when he gave her that really understanding look. That's my understanding look, not hers. Mine."

Castiel frowned. "No, not then, honey. I mean now. Today. Do you remember being shot today?"

I pursed my lips and tried to make my mind switch gears. "Yes. Kind of. Linc and Conleigh were standing in front of me while we walked to the car. I was standing behind because I was texting Wade to let him know we were on the way home and Conleigh had to poop. Did you know Conleigh won't poop anywhere but her house? Apparently, it really is a phobia that she's just recently acquired. A reporter followed her into the bathroom without her knowing it and she pooped, and it was all on that news channel, AMZ, CMT…something like that."

"Honey," Castiel said, a smile on his face. "The shooting. Do you remember who shot you?"

I glared at him. "I was getting there, Reaper!"

Castiel held up his hands in surrender. "Sorry, sorry. I'll try not to interrupt."

I glared. "You just do that."

I felt the bed shaking, but since I was a focused individual, I chose not to acknowledge it and instead continued my narrative.

"Anyway, we stopped for a snack. I'm always hungry. We had some Subway, and Conleigh got a cookie. Linc told her not to get it because that particular kind always made her stomach hurt. But she got it anyway. And what do you know? She had to poop like fifteen minutes later, so we were going to go ahead and go. I was texting Wade about leaving when I must've gotten separated from Linc and Conleigh. I looked up and all of a sudden, I'm staring at a woman—the grandmother of one of my kiddos from the daycare—and she was pointing a gun at me. She was actually wearing a black ski mask kind of pulled up, but I could tell who it was from her body, her hands. She has this weird mole on the back of her left hand that looks like a pile of dog poop. Plus, she was with her daughter, Debbie Schultz, who I could see was in the car waiting for her—though she wasn't wearing a mask."

I paused, thinking about it. "I dropped my cookie in the parking lot. Man, I really wanted that cookie." I turned to see Wade staring at me with a thunderous expression on his face. "Will you go get me a cookie?"

He blinked, and the thunderous expression was gone. "Yes, baby. What kind was it?"

"It was a double-stacked piece of cookie cake from the Cookie Factory. The top part had white icing on it, and the middle part had pink icing in it. That's important. They have to be the same kind, and look the same, too. Conleigh!" I cried out.

"Right here, sweetheart," Conleigh called, smiling wide.

I frowned at her. "I hope you didn't poop your pants. That would've been very awkward."

She opened her mouth and then closed it just as quickly. "No, I didn't. That urge left me really fast when everything happened."

The certainty in her words made me relax. "Oh, good. After all that you told me about the paparazzi, I was so worried you'd shit yourself and then it'd be on the cameras. What happened to your forehead?"

She pointed at her husband, who didn't look the least bit sorry for hurting his wife.

"This man right here tackled me to the ground. It hurt really, really bad." She paused. "I asked him to do that to me once, and he said no. Now I understand why he told me no."

With that ringing in my ears, I went to sleep.

Lani Lynn Vale

CHAPTER 18

Sometimes you have to be the bigger person and walk away. Just kidding. Turn around and knock that mofo's teeth out.

-Wade to Landry

Wade

"I can't decide whether to laugh or cry," Linc said softly the moment Landry's eyes closed.

I closed my eyes as I replayed the last two hours in my head. Like a goddamn bad record on repeat, with the same fucked up problem every single time it started over.

"Hello?" I answered the phone.

"Got a problem. Shooting at the mall. Your woman was shot in the belly. She's on the way to the hospital," Bayou growled over the line.

The next five minutes had been the longest of my life.

I'd made that trip to the hospital hundreds, no, thousands, of time. It'd always seemed so short.

But all of the times that I'd gone, it'd never been Landry in trouble. It'd always been someone else.

Never her.

I'd driven like a maniac, and I prayed the whole way that she'd be okay.

Generally, I wasn't a religious man. I believed in God, but I also believed in proven facts.

Then, I hadn't been able to prove a goddamn thing. All I could do was pray. So, that's what I did.

Possible liver laceration. Severe concussion. Blood loss.

The list of her injuries were numerous, but the one that was the most worrisome was the liver damage.

"We're going to take her up to the OR now," someone said, causing me to blink and yank myself out of my head.

"What?"

"We have to assess the damage to her liver, and we're going to remove the bullet," the doctor said. He paused. "If you know anyone with AB negative blood, get them in here. We worked four traumas over the last six hours, and we haven't been able to replenish our blood supply yet. O negative will work in a pinch."

And that was how I found myself in the OR waiting room with my entire MC, waiting to hear the outcome of my wife's surgery.

It was two hours into my wait when loud footsteps caused me to look up. Only it wasn't the doctor like I was hoping. It was Castiel.

He looked pissed, too.

He'd left earlier once Landry had been able to identify her gunman. From there I hadn't thought about him again until then, my thoughts too focused on Landry and whether she was okay.

But now, seeing the angry scowl on Castiel's face, I stood up as I felt exhilaration start to race through my blood.

"Did you find her?" I called.

I hadn't meant to say it as loud as I did, but I was too hopeful that he had.

"I did," Castiel confirmed. "At her house, wrestling in the front yard with her daughter."

I frowned. "What?"

Castiel nodded once. "You heard me right. They're both pretty banged up…so I brought them here."

I smiled for the first time since I'd gotten the call that my wife had been shot.

Moving swiftly to the young woman that was manning the front desk—the one in charge of letting people know how their loved ones are or if there were any updates to be had—I stopped in front of her and said, "I'll be downstairs. Will you please call me if there are any updates?"

The woman nodded. "I have your number on file, sir."

I'd already been up to talk to her eight times. She was likely happy to see me go.

"Thank you," I replied gruffly.

And, as one, nearly eighty-five percent of the waiting room got up with me.

I held out my hand to them. "Stay."

The men snorted, but Conleigh and Izzy retook their seats—both side by side.

The men followed me, and honestly, I couldn't find it in me to care.

I liked that they wanted to be there, and I liked even more that I had their support.

Taking long, fast steps, I didn't once notice the bite of pain in my leg, nor did I notice how angry I looked.

If I'd been thinking more clearly, I likely would've tried to control the look on my face, or change my body language to not give away my murderous intentions.

Instead, I barreled down the hall, only stopping long enough at the elevator to find out what floor they were on from Castiel.

Unlucky for me, they were in the ER, which was filled with too many people for me to really do the damage that I wanted to.

But, I was going to do what I had to do to. Right then, I wasn't a cop. I wasn't a nice person. I was a man, who had just seen the aftermath of his wife being shot by a woman who didn't realize who she was messing with.

I was about to show her.

And none of the men at my back were going to stop me.

I came to a stop outside of the curtain where the two women responsible for this entire shit storm were located. I was contemplating walking in there and wrapping my hands around the throat of the woman that had been the reason for all my pain and agony over the last few hours but held myself in check.

Barely.

"Shut up, Debbie," the woman snarled. "This is all your fault. If you'd focused on doing it the right way, and not being a goddamn dumbass, this might've all worked out the way it was supposed to. And for God's sake, stop worrying about the goddamn dog that she stole. Worry about the fact that you'll never see your babies again."

"My husband will bring them to see me in prison," she said. "Have you never seen that show on Netflix?"

"I don't think you're understanding the gravity of this situation," Debbie's mother hissed. "This is not a goddamn TV show. This is real-fucking-life. I shot someone today!"

"Shh," Debbie whispered too loudly. "If you don't admit it…"

I'd heard enough.

The two imbeciles behind the curtain obviously thought they were in a private room or something. They weren't.

I yanked the partition away and stared at the two women.

One was someone I'd seen quite a few times before she stopped coming into the daycare. I'd often gone to visit my wife during the rush hour of dropping kids off in the morning. Debbie. The other was obviously Debbie's mother. Hannelore Petty.

They both clammed up tight at the sight of me—not to mention the other men at my back.

Their eyes were jumping in between each other at a high rate of speed.

Had anything in this situation been funny, it would be the look on their faces at seeing me.

Unfortunately, I wasn't in the laughing mood.

"You shot my wife," I said to Hannelore.

Hannelore didn't say a word, but her eyes did flare.

"No, she didn't," Debbie lied. "Someone else did."

I didn't spare the idiot a glance. My eyes were all for the mother.

"You thought that *what*? You'd get away with it?" I questioned.

She still said nothing.

"She was watching my kids all day," Debbie said. "I was also at home. You can check my ankle monitor status."

It'd been checked the moment that things had settled down enough for everyone to think rationally. After Castiel made sure that Landry had made it to the hospital alive, he'd immediately set out to investigating the whereabouts of Debbie—who surprisingly had been released on bail that morning.

Unfortunately, her alibi had been easy to check out because she did, indeed, have an ankle monitor. The judge had deemed her a flight risk and made the monitor a condition of her bail—which had been posted by her mother. Surprise.

I wonder if that'd been her mother's goal, to have Debbie do the dirty work. It was possible that she hadn't known about the monitor when she'd bailed her out. I hadn't known about it.

I also hadn't known that she'd gotten out. Though that was easily explained by Castiel, who'd informed me that he'd had someone monitoring her twenty-four seven, and there was no way in hell that she was going to slip past them.

Which, I suppose, she hadn't.

"It's already been checked, and you did leave your house," Castiel came to stand beside me. "In addition, we've had a positive identification on both of you. Once we get you cleaned up, Ms. Petty, we'll be taking you to county lock-up for the attempted murder of Landry Johnson."

Hannelore's mouth fell open in shock. "You can't pin anything on me!"

"Yeah," Debbie said. "She wore a mask. You can't pin anything on her."

She seriously couldn't be that stupid, could she?

"What color mask?" Castiel asked inquiringly.

"It was black. I bought it off of Amazon during hunting season last year. It has a really cute Under Armour symbol right here." She pointed to her forehead.

"Like this one?" Castiel asked.

Hannelore was shouting "I'm going to kill you with my bare hands" vibes at her daughter, but Debbie seemed clueless.

It wasn't until Castiel pulled out a folded piece of paper that showed the mask—symbol exactly where it was—on Hannelore's face. The best angle Castiel had been able to find was one of a side profile shot with Hannelore tugging it down over her face. The only thing visible was her hairy goddamn chin.

"That is the one," Debbie confirmed.

Castiel looked at me. "Why did we allow her to continue visiting with her children?"

It was more than obvious that he thought Debbie was an imbecile.

I happened to agree with him.

But, since it was giving us what we wanted, I couldn't fault Debbie for being a dumbass.

Debbie shot me a smug look, and I balled my fist up tightly to keep myself from doing or saying anything that might get me sent to jail right along with them.

Luckily, before I could act on the urges and desires that were running through my veins, my phone rang, interrupting the tense silence now happening around us.

The moment I placed it to my ear, I could hear the caution in the volunteer's voice that was on the other end of the line. "Um, Mr. Johnson? This is the volunteer that works in surgery? The doctor just called and gave me an update. They finished."

She didn't give me anything more, and I had a feeling I wasn't going to like the reason why.

"I'll be back as soon as I can," I told the girl. "Thank you."

The girl didn't wait for a reply. I didn't give her the time of day.

My mind was now completely on Landry.

"You're okay here?" I asked Castiel.

I trusted the man with my life.

Castiel nodded once. "Yes. I'll keep you updated."

With that, I took him at his word and walked quickly to the elevator, not sparing those two obviously stupid women even a backward glance.

I didn't turn around until I was in the elevator and all of the men traipsed on with me.

"Your wife," Rome said softly. "She's a tough cookie. She'll be just fine."

Unfortunately, his words couldn't be further from the truth.

CHAPTER 19

Whatever sprinkles your donut.

-Coffee Cup

Wade

"The bullet entered here," the doctor said, going over an x-ray that was taken sometime yesterday when she'd been brought in. "When we did surgery, we found that the liver lost blood supply for quite a while. Unfortunately, parts of the liver were already dead, and we had to do a resection. We're also not sure if what we were able to save will, in fact, survive. The first forty-eight hours is going to be the deciding factor. If she makes it through then, she'll likely have a very good chance of making it. Though, I think we should still get her on the donor registry…just in case."

"What does that mean?" my mother asked softly.

My mother and father had arrived in the middle of the night and had come straight here the moment they'd heard the news.

My mom and dad were sitting on the small loveseat in the corner of the room while I stood beside Landry's bedside, holding her hand.

Landry had been asleep on and off since she'd woken from surgery a little over seven hours ago. This was actually the first time the doctor had been back since I'd spoken with him briefly after the surgery.

"It means," Dr. Tibil said quietly. "That we need to get her on the transplant list in case the part of the liver we were able to save fails."

Those words hung in the air.

"Livers can be split in half, right? If one of us were matches, we could donate to her, correct?" my mother asked, sitting forward in her seat.

"Yes," he agreed. "But with all the damage that her body has gone through after losing her right kidney as well, her body is very weak. If she doesn't have a perfect match, then it's likely that her body will just reject it."

I closed my eyes and felt that there was only one thing that I could do.

It was Landry who stopped me. "Don't you dare."

I looked down at my wife, who was watching me with knowing eyes.

"Don't I dare what?" I asked, knowing she knew me better than I sometimes knew myself.

"Ask her," she whispered. "Don't. Please don't."

I smiled. "We're going to get tested first. Then, we'll explore other options if there's not a match. But baby, we may not even need it. You may be just fine."

She narrowed her eyes at me. "I don't want to ask her for anything."

"Now, I've put in a request to have more blood, AB negative, delivered to the hospital. Have you all been tested to make sure you're not a match?" the doctor asked.

"Yes. We did that one by one just a few hours ago. None of us are matches. Castiel was O negative and was able to donate two pints. I believe that's what you got while you were in surgery."

The doctor nodded at my words. "Put the word out." He looked at Landry. "She could use some more."

With that he left, leaving my heart in my throat.

***

I felt no such compunction.

Walking up the front walk to Landry's parents' home, I knew that this meeting wasn't going to go well.

Not after what I'd learned about her parents once Landry opened up to me when we'd found out that we were still married.

I knocked sharply, unwilling to stop myself from taking this step despite the fact that I knew it would piss Landry off greatly.

The big red doors didn't even flinch at the pounding of my knuckles against the expensive wood.

Lina was surprisingly the one to answer the door.

Honestly, I'd been expecting a butler or something with how big the place was.

"Wade!" Lina grinned. "How are you?"

Her smile faltered as she took in the expression on my face.

"Not good, Lina," I said softly. "Landry was shot last night."

Lina's mouth dropped open, and the open devastation on her face wasn't altered or faked. It was real. There was no doubt in my mind about that.

"What happened?" she whispered, her eyes filling with fear.

I looked down at my hands, unwilling to be swayed to her side this time.

"I know you may hate your sister," I started. "But she's given you a lot. So fucking much. She donated life to you six times." I paused. "Now it might possibly be your turn."

Her eyes narrowed. "What are you talking about? And, of course I don't hate her…she hates me. Despite that, I'd do anything for her." She looked away. "She's just never asked."

The bad thing was, this was what got me the first time. The pure sincerity in her voice let me know that she really felt what she'd been saying to be true.

She sounded like she meant every word she said.

And honestly, it was too good to be true.

But while she was feeling charitable, I was going to grab the bull by the horns…or the sister by the hand. I was getting her the fuck out of there before she changed her mind.

CHAPTER 20

Douche.

-Wade to a suspect

Wade

"I used to write her letters," Lina hiccupped. "God, I used to pray that she'd come play with me. Something…anything. But she never came."

I turned my attention from Landry, who'd been asleep since we'd gotten there, and Lina.

"From the stories that Landry has told me, she didn't have a choice. Your mother wouldn't let her anywhere near you." He paused. "Landry always told me that you didn't like her, not the other way around."

A sharp knock at the door had us all turning to see who was there.

It was the doctor, and he had a happy, pleased smile on his face.

"You were right. Perfect match," Dr. Tibil said solemnly. "Unfortunately, you neglected to mention that you were recovering from cancer. I'm sorry, but you won't be able to donate any of your liver. I'm sorry." He paused. "Your blood, however? That we can take. As long as you feel up to it."

I looked over at Lina who looked completely devastated. "Are you sure?"

"I'm sure," he said, voice filled with sorrow. "But, as of right now, she's doing very, very well. She's done remarkably well, and with another pint of blood in her? She'll start bouncing back far more quickly. Trust me."

Dr. Tibil clapped me on the back, a sharp crack to fill the room, causing me to flick my eyes over to Landry to see if that'd woken her.

It hadn't.

She looked awful, and she was starting to get a yellowish sheen to her skin and around her mouth.

The doctor said that was normal due to the buildup of bilirubin that her liver was having a harder time filtering out, but as soon as the body was able to catch up, that yellowish tint would disappear.

In fact, over the past few hours as he'd been observing her, he'd been pleasantly surprised with Landry's progress.

I felt a weird sort of questioning in my chest.

Surely, it wasn't that easy.

Surely, things were about to go badly.

Landry and me? We just weren't that fucking lucky.

"All right, I'll get a nurse in here to put you on tap, so to speak." He left the room without another word.

Lina turned to me, but I didn't take my eyes away from Landry, who was lying so fucking still.

"She's going to kill me for asking you," I whispered. "She's so fucking sure that you've been a part of making her life hell, Lina. Please tell me that I'm not involving you just for you to turn around and hurt her."

Lina was quiet for a few long seconds. "I want to know my sister. I've always wanted to know her. I follow her around, hoping to work up the courage to talk to her, and never quite seem to find it. It's hard when my parents tell me how much she hates me."

I snorted. "Funny, but it seems like both your parents are doing that to each of you at the same time. Don't you find it odd that y'all can't seem to get along long enough to talk it out?"

The one and only time I'd seen the two together in the same vicinity of one another, it hadn't lasted long because they'd both immediately gone on the defensive.

"God," she whispered. "It's no wonder she hates me. I ruined her childhood, and my parents always chose my side over hers."

Before I could tell her that her parents had, indeed, been part of the problem, said parents walked in the door.

They didn't stop to knock. Didn't stop to greet us. They walked straight in, briefly swept their eyes over a too-still Landry, and focused on their other daughter. The favorite.

"You will not do this," Lina's mother ordered. "I didn't spend eighteen years of my life making sure that you were healthy to have you throw it away now."

Lina's eyes narrowed on her mother, not correcting them in their obviously misguided assumptions that she was donating part of her liver to Landry. "You think donating half of my liver to my sister is throwing my life away?"

Lina and Landry's mother, Vienna, lifted her lip in a silent snarl. Moments later, she turned to her husband with a disgusting scowl on her face. "You fix this. Fix it now, or you'll be sorry."

With that, she walked until she was standing just outside the room, leaving Lina sitting beside Landry's bed, and me standing in between her chair and Landry's. Lina and Landry's father, Albert, standing by the door, seconds away from leaving the room as well.

He looked sad…and tired.

"Dad?" Lina whispered. "What's the problem here? This is Landry. This is my sister. What the hell is going on?"

If Lina hadn't looked unaffected by the entire debacle, I might have been in a different state of mind and forced Albert from the room just to make sure that Albert didn't have a chance to change anyone's mind about helping Landry.

But Lina was so determined to help I didn't think anything would change her mind.

"I can't do this anymore," Albert said, looking at the bed Landry was lying in with a look of defeat on his face. "God, I just can't." He took a deep breath and blew it out harshly before beginning to speak. "Landry was a mistake," Albert whispered. "She's your half-sister, not your real sister. And despite what we allowed y'all to think, Landry was conceived the all-natural way…only she wasn't conceived with your mother. She was conceived by me and another woman—your mother's sister."

Out of all the things I'd been expecting him to say, that hadn't been it.

"Senna, your mother's sister, died a couple years after Landry was born. We didn't know about it until Landry arrived with a note from Senna. Senna had died from cancer, and her nanny had delivered her to our front porch. About two days before that, you were so goddamn sick…it was a fluke that y'all were matches. Kismet. That's the only reason that your mother agreed for her to stay."

And then it all made a sick sort of sense.

Why Landry was hated so much by her mother. Why Landry had been treated like a stepchild. Why Landry had been kept away from her sister.

Why, ultimately, she was treated like she didn't belong.

"Get out," I said to them both. "Get out, and don't come back."

"You can't kick me out of my own daughter's hospital room," Albert stiffened.

I laughed. "Is she your daughter? Because honestly, to me, it seems like you treated her more as a person that held the key to keeping your wife happy. As long as Landry was useful to have around, she was allowed to stay. The moment she became not useful to you, she was tossed aside, treated as if she wasn't worth the effort." I snarled. "Well let me tell you something, mother fucker. Landry's worth it. You've missed out on everything, and you have nobody to blame for it but yourself."

Albert took a step back at the vehemence in my voice.

Vienna snorted from the hallway through the partially open door and called out. "We'll go. Come, Lina."

Lina shook her head. "Not this time, Mom." She paused. "What did you do with my letters that I wrote to Landry?"

Vienna scowled as she poked her head back in the hospital room. "Put them somewhere that wouldn't disrupt the system. Now, you either come with me, or everything changes for you. You can find someone else to pay for your medical bills, and someone else to make sure that you're always safe. If you let that girl in your life, you are no longer my blood."

I felt like snarling. I was seconds away from beating the shit out of an older woman.

What kind of cop and man did that?

One who was supremely pissed off and wanted the trash out of his wife's hospital room.

"She can stay with us," Castiel said, surprising me. "I'll take care of her."

Lina looked over at Castiel like he was a leper. "No way am I staying with you, death angel. Not after what you accused me of a week ago."

I frowned, wondering what it was that they were speaking of.

"Alright," a nurse came in. "You and you, leave. You, sit down so I can start. You, why are you even here?" that was directed at Castiel, who'd arrived somewhere in between the explanation from Albert. "You, go to the corner of the room and stop being such a big space taker."

I did as I was told, and watched quietly as Lina donated a pint of blood for her sister.

CHAPTER 21

A large group of people is called a 'no thanks.'

-Coffee Cup

Landry

"Funny, I don't remember consenting to that!" I snarled.

It was a pitiful snarl, of course, but it was a snarl nonetheless.

"Funny, I don't remember giving you a choice," Lina retorted. "Now, shut up and enjoy my blood. I'm trying to sleep."

Unfortunately for Lina and for me, after she'd donated the pint of blood, she'd gotten woozy and hadn't been able to get up from the couch where she'd planted herself afterward. Every time she tried to get up, she became dizzy and so nauseous that she threw up. At least, that was what Castiel and Wade had informed me.

"Why are you so calm about this?" I finally growled. "You ruined my childhood, and you were going to casually give me half your liver like you weren't the worst sister ever?"

"Me?" Lina asked. "I wasn't the worst sister ever! You were! Would it have hurt you to come visit me every once in a while?"

I frowned at that. "What do you mean? You told me not to visit you. I especially remember that when we were older. In fact, the last time you told me to leave and never come back was before you graduated from high school. You screamed at me. Sister or not, you can't come back from that."

Lina got this funny look on her face. "I told you not to come back because you were giving me a pity visit. The only reason you came in there was because my mother asked you to bring me something. Would it have killed you to walk in there and say 'hi' when you weren't asked to?"

I frowned. "Mom told me that you didn't want me there."

Lina laughed, and the laughter contained zero trace of humor. In fact, she sounded quite pissed.

"My mother is a dick wad," Lina said.

"Why do you keep referring to her as your mother and not 'our' mother?" I finally asked. "You've decided to no longer allow me claim to her?"

I mean, technically, I didn't really want all that much to do with her anyway, but still, she was all I had.

Not that it was a good thing to have most of the time. But it seemed to piss our mother off when I spoke of her as being related to me, so I was going to keep that and own it—just to piss her off more.

"Landry," Wade said softly, bringing my gaze to his face. "I think it's time we had a talk. Since you're well enough to hold a twenty-five-minute never-ending argument, I think it's time you hear what we have to say."

I frowned.

Wade had been asking me if I was 'alert' all day long. If I could understand where I was, and what had happened.

All of those answers had apparently not been enough for him, which I hadn't really cared about since I'd been so tired and weak.

However, after getting some apple juice and some beef broth in me, I felt like a new woman.

A new woman that had her sister in her hospital room with her that also so happened to have apparently given me blood that had caused her to pass out and not move for hours.

I didn't want her blood in me! I'd take anybody's blood but hers!

The look on Wade's face made me pause in concern.

He was looking at me like I wasn't going to like what he had to say.

"Anyway, I've learned some interesting things over the past forty-nine and a half hours," he started, causing Lina to snort in amusement.

I glowered at her before returning my gaze back to Wade's face.

"And?" I said impatiently.

My side was starting to hurt with all this talking—as the nurse had said it would—but I didn't stop myself. Only continued to stare at the man sitting in the chair beside my bed.

"And when I went to ask Lina if she'd be willing to donate half her liver—" I couldn't let that go without a derisive snort. "She came straight here. Unfortunately, the doctor denied her because of her cancer background. Her mother, however, learned that she was here as well…" I groaned at his use of 'her mother' as Lina had been saying over the last hour. "And she came up here and confronted us."

My brows lifted in surprise. "No shit?"

She nodded once. "No shit."

"Then let's get this over with. What did they say?" I asked.

I was assuming it was bad because Lina was wincing with sympathy, and Wade looked like he'd rather cut his leg off than tell me.

"Dear God, just spit it out already!"

Castiel, who'd been occupying the seat in the corner, was the one to say it.

"Your father fucked your mother's sister, got her pregnant, and then didn't find out about you until your mother died. The only reason your mother allowed you to stay in her house without throwing an unholy bitch fit was due to your sister having a disease that only you could cure with your bone marrow. Since your father was used to the cushy lifestyle that your mother's trust fund financed and didn't want to be separated from his sick daughter, he went along with his wife's demands. Which was, in essence, to alienate you. Your father's conditions were simple. She couldn't harm you or tell you that you weren't hers. As long as you weren't seriously harmed in any way he was okay with everything else."

Wade cursed under his breath just as Castiel cursed.

I blinked as my sister smacked him upside the head. Lina groaned as she started to laugh at Castiel's glare.

I stared at everyone in confusion.

Then started to laugh myself.

"Then, let me get this straight," I said carefully, trying to control my hilarity despite it causing me pain. "I was shot by a grandmother whose daughter burned my house down. A woman who has also been stealing dogs out from under my nose and murdering them when they easily have at least a year or two of good quality life left. My father admitted that she wasn't actually my mother—my actual mother being deceased. My father allowed me to be emotionally abused, but not physically abused, over the course of my lifetime. My sister doesn't actually hate me like I've thought she's hated me seeing as she willingly donated me a pint of her blood. Oh, and I'm still married when I thought I wasn't. All in about a month's time. Do I have this correct?"

Almost as if they'd planned it out, everyone in the room nodded—even Pru, the nurse who was standing next to Hoax.

Why the nurse was there, I didn't know.

But she wasn't actually my nurse any longer.

She and Hoax were standing side by side whispering about something, small smiles on both of their faces.

My sister was wiping her eyes with her hands, but a smile was solidly on her face.

My husband was looking at me like he wanted to kiss me.

And then there was Hoax, who was looking at me like I was finally getting some inside joke or secret that I wasn't understanding before.

"Yep," Hoax agreed. "That's what I hear, anyway."

That's when I, too, started to laugh.

And it hurt.

Like a mother fucker.

Lani Lynn Vale

CHAPTER 22

My spirit animal would fuckin' eat yours.

-Landry to Wade

Wade

I crossed my arms over my chest and stared at the lawyer that was appointed by the state for Mrs. Petty, the woman who'd almost stolen my wife's life.

"Your honor," the lawyer tried to interrupt.

"I'm sorry, but the doctor has spoken. The jury has spoken. And I have spoken. There's no longer a choice in the matter. Mrs. Petty is not clinically insane. She was more than aware of her misdeeds." He slammed his gavel on the desk then stood up. "Case closed."

That's when he stood and walked out of the courtroom, disappearing through a door along the side of the room.

Moments after he was gone, the officer in charge of the court walked over with a set of handcuffs, which he deftly slipped onto the lying cow's wrists.

Moments after that, she was taken from the room as well.

Landry looked from the now-closed door to me, and then back again.

"She got everything we'd hoped for," she whispered in awe.

I grinned. "People don't take kindly to cop's wives being shot at. You're part of the LEO—law enforcement officer—family. Plus, Judge Painter doesn't pull his punches. I had a feeling he wasn't going to go easy on her."

Mrs. Petty had received twenty-eight years in prison with a possibility of parole at eighteen years. By that point, she'd be eighty-three, and likely unable to do anything in retaliation once she got out.

If she made it out.

Older females didn't make it long in prison for some reason. Which was my secret hope.

Not that I'd be telling anybody that.

"Well, we couldn't have asked for a better outcome," my Uncle Jimmy said as he stood. "Now. What do you think…."

"We're staying married," I cut him off at the same time that Landry said, "He's mine. No one can have him."

I grinned at my wife.

My uncle rolled his eyes. "I was going to say what do you think you want to eat for lunch?"

I rolled my eyes.

Landry seemed to seriously consider it.

"I want a steak," my father said, sidling up to us.

"I'd love a good Porterhouse," Hoax said, his arm around the blonde nurse.

It'd been a little over two and a half months since Landry had been shot, and during that month, life had changed a lot for us.

We'd started building our own house in a new subdivision in town, and it was about halfway finished.

Debbie Shultz had been tried and sentenced to a mental health facility where she would remain until she was stable enough to go to prison for ten years for arson.

Debbie's ex-husband, Mal, had moved two states over with his children so they'd be "away from the crazy" according to him.

Kourt, after finding out all that had gone down with Landry, had understandably been suspicious of Lina's motives and had set about proving her wrong.

All he'd done was prove her right, especially when he'd snuck into their parents' place and found a few stray letters that Lina had written to Landry stuffed in her mother's jewelry box.

It was only a matter of time now until those two were fucking each other.

At first, I'd thought that she and Castiel would possibly get something going, but it quickly became apparent that Castiel and Lina were more of a brother and sister type relationship rather than romantically.

Landry's parents had made zero attempts at reconciliation with either of the two girls.

Which worked for me. If they never came back, I'd be happy.

Especially since, now that the two crazy people after my woman were gone, we were about to start the next chapter of our life.

We'd also started looking into adoption.

At least, I had.

Landry was scared shitless and wanted nothing at all to do with it.

I, on the other hand, wouldn't allow her to be ruled by her fears.

Which had been why I'd started to discreetly inquire about adoption loans, because goddamn was it expensive.

I'd succeeded in securing one that was meant for law enforcement families seeking to adopt, and the next step was actually contacting an agency.

I just had to convince my wife to take that step.

"The steak place is open," Kourt suggested, coming up to stand next to Lina, I suspected, just to annoy her.

"Ohhhh," Pru groaned. "The rolls from there are divine. And the sweet tea. Oh, and the macaroni. Now I'm starving, and we have to go there."

Landry snorted and stood up. "You had me at rolls."

I grinned and pulled her to me, placing a soft kiss on her forehead.

"You okay, baby?"

She nodded at me, looking like she was free of chains for the first time in a long time.

"Yeah," she agreed. "I'm perfect."

Before I could say another word, she buried her face in my armpit and continued to walk, effectively putting an end to our conversation.

"Y'all don't mind if my sister comes, do you?" Pru asked. "She's crazy busy these days, and I like to make sure that she eats."

"No problem," Hoax said. "We can swing by and pick…never mind. We're on my bike."

"I'll do it," Bayou offered.

"I'll go pick Izzy and the baby up, and then we'll meet you there," Rome said as he slapped me on the back.

After returning the slap, he left, and the rest of us followed.

It was then that I realized that life was back to normal for me.

I'd returned to work last week—on regular duty.

My leg, although still healing, was finally showing improvement now that the infection had been controlled. There were still days that it ached, but I could run on it. I could pivot and stretch. Hell, I could even fuck Landry in the shower without dropping her.

In my book, that counted as a win.

"Let's go eat, babe." Landry poked me in the side.

I blinked, unsure when I'd stopped.

We were standing at the top of the courthouse steps, and there wasn't a single person around us anymore. They'd all walked toward their respective bikes and had started off.

I dropped my gaze and turned my head so that I was staring into her eyes.

And I knew that later, I'd broach the subject that she'd been avoiding.

I just hoped that I didn't hurt her in the process.

Hours later, after a good meal with family and friends, I finally worked up the courage.

And what I got in reply to my question wasn't the one I was hoping for.

But it was the one that was real.

Which was what I wanted. What we needed.

"I'm just not ready yet, Wade," she whispered to me later that night when I yet again raised the issue. "I don't know if I'll ever be ready."

I dropped my mouth to hers, deepening the kiss so that she realized that I wasn't upset about her insecurities. If we never had kids, that was okay.

As long as I had her, it would be enough.

And I showed her that with my body.

With my mouth worshipping every inch of her skin. With my tongue lathing her breasts, and her pussy.

With each and every hard, rough stroke of my cock.

With each caress and squeeze.

And when we came together long minutes later, both of us breathless and replete, I knew that it was all that mattered.

Here. Now.

Her.

EPILOGUE

I didn't ask who put it there. I said pick it up.

-Things I repeat eight million times a day to my kid.

Wade

"I don't know what to do with them, man," someone said softly.

I looked over to find Castiel, a sleeping two-year-old against his chest, staring at me like he was about to be sick to his stomach.

Me, with a newly born baby girl resting on mine, was feeling the exact same thing.

The baby that I was holding had been delivered only two minutes before—by me and Castiel.

Medics hadn't even had a chance to arrive yet.

"Have Landry meet us at the hospital," I said softly. "CPS—child protective services—said that they'd be here in an hour and a half. You can call them and tell them that you moved both kids to the hospital to be checked out. The CPS chick knows Landry. She won't mind."

Castiel looked relieved to finally have a solution.

Me, on the other hand, I was on my way to the hospital with the mother and newborn.

Unfortunately for the mother, she'd fucked up. Big time.

How had she fucked up?

She'd thought it was the greatest idea in the world to rob a bank with her boyfriend while her two-year-old sat in the car waiting for them to come out.

In the excitement of robbing the bank, she'd gone into labor.

A car chase had ensued, and when the car had wrecked and been too fucked up to keep driving, the man had bailed.

The mother had at least stopped to grab the two-year-old, but she hadn't made it far before we'd caught up to her just as her contractions had taken her down.

We'd found her so quickly because we'd been hot on their tails—they weren't exactly a modern-day Bonnie and Clyde.

The other cruiser had followed the boyfriend while Castiel and I had stopped to help the mother—who'd been in the middle of an intersection with cars all around her and a two-year-old scared out of his mind.

And, before we could even move them out of the street, she'd started pushing.

I'd been aware enough to catch the baby before it'd fallen to the hot ground.

"Landry will know what to do."

***

When I got home hours later, well past dark, it was to find Landry on the couch watching television with Capo resting against her feet in the cushion that was normally my spot.

The newest addition—a sixteen-year-old sheepdog named Tooter—rested against the wall in the foyer.

Stepping over the old pup, I walked directly to Landry and leaned over her to drop a kiss on her mouth.

"I'm going to take a shower."

Minutes after stripping out of my clothes, I was under the spray of the water, trying hard to figure out what in the fuck had just happened.

The mother had given up rights to both of her kids, signed them away as if they were nothing more than inconvenient pieces of trash.

"Wade?"

I swallowed and opened my eyes to find her staring at my worriedly.

"You okay?" she asked softly.

I shrugged. "That mother just gave her kids up like they were Pokémon cards to trade. The DA offered it as a joke, and she took it."

Landry's eyes went hard.

"The boy? He was covered in bruises. He was malnourished. There were so many scabs, cuts, and scrapes on him that I would've called CPS myself had he come in as one of my kids. She wasn't a mother to him. It was the best thing that could ever happen to him—her giving him up."

I looked down, letting the water cascade over the back of my neck.

"Here we are, unable to have kids, and wanting them so badly that our hearts hurt. Then there's her. Having them easily—apparently, she'd had five abortions before, she was happy to point that out—and doesn't even want them. How is that fucking fair?"

Landry walked into the shower, clothes and all, wrapping her arms around me.

"I don't know, Wade. I just don't know."

***

Landry

It was two hours later that I made the call.

"Hey, Shiloh," I said softly. "I need to talk to you about a couple of babies."

***

Two days later

"Where are we going?" Wade grumbled. "Fuck, but I just wanted to sleep in."

I felt my lips twitch.

"Oh, we just have to go pick something up," I murmured, heart pounding.

"At the hospital?" he asked warily. "What in the hell would be there that I would need to pick up?"

I rolled my eyes. "Why can't you just drive me there?"

"And why did we have to take the truck?" he grumbled. "I hate driving the truck when it's such nice weather outside."

I sighed in exasperation. "Seriously, what in the fuck is your problem?"

I knew what his problem was.

He'd been in a bad mood since the delivery of that baby a few days ago. He'd been acting like an angry bull ever since.

"Nothing," he grumbled, going stoically silent for the rest of the ride.

I kept my smile in check and directed him where to go.

"There," I said, pointing. "Where that cart and all those balloons are. With the big box. There."

Wade did as I said.

"What's in the box?" he asked, pushing the door open.

I looked out the open car window to see Shiloh Allen, the CPS agent that I knew well, standing there smiling wide.

"A car seat," Shiloh answered him.

I got out of the car at the same time that a mini-van pulled up behind us.

Minnie and Porter.

Perfect timing.

"Mom?" Wade stopped beside all the flowers. "What the fuck?"

That's when the screaming of an infant broke the quiet morning air, causing us all to turn and stare at a nurse who was rolling out a baby—who was being held by Castiel in a wheelchair.

Wade frowned.

"I don't know what's going on right now."

"You're being deliberately obtuse, son." Porter strolled around the van and opened the car door. It was then that the two-year-old, with his healing bruises and a cup of chocolate milk, was revealed. "And I think it all has to do with the fact that you're too afraid to hope."

Wade turned to me, and a look of such hope and pleading entered his eyes that I felt like a big piece of crap for thinking to deny my man anything because of my insecurities.

"Landry," Wade whispered.

I smiled as I felt tears form in my eyes. "We're only their foster parents for now, but Shiloh has already started on the paperwork for the adoption process. In three to six months, they'll officially be ours."

Wade dropped his head and contemplated his feet for a few long seconds before lifting it back up and staring at me with unaltered happiness in his eyes. "This is the fourth best day of my life."

I smiled.

"What was the first?" Castiel asked as he stood up, eyes wide and a little freaked out.

Bayou, who'd come from somewhere in the parking lot, started to rip into the box that was holding the car seat.

In a matter of moments, he had it all unwrapped and headed to our truck.

"The day that I married her," Wade answered. "And before you ask the next two, it was the day I met her, and then the day I found out that we were still married that fill out the other two."

Tears tipped over the edge and started to streak down my face.

"Here," Castiel said when the baby started to really belt out her frustration. "I can't deal with this."

Wade didn't hesitate.

He walked over to Cass, picked the baby up in his arms, and then cuddled her up to his big, muscular chest.

I felt something clog my throat at the sight.

"We'll just leave this big guy in our car on the way home," Porter said. "We'll transfer over the seat and the shit—I mean stuff—when we get to your place."

"Car seat is in," Bayou rumbled.

"Perfect!" Shiloh clapped. "I have a lot of stuff in this box here for y'all. Formula, diapers, clothes. Donations of all kinds that should hold you through the day. I'm so excited for y'all."

I looked over at my longtime friend.

I'd had to call her twice now since I'd started to run my own daycare, and I never thought I'd see the day that she'd be giving me a gift such as this.

Wade moved until he was standing directly in front of me, his eyes so intently focused on mine that I could practically feel his emotions.

"You just made my life, woman."

I stood up on tippy toes, one hand going to his chest, and the other going to the little girl's tiny back and pressed my lips to his.

"It's only fair since you made mine, too."

ABOUT THE AUTHOR

Lani Lynn Vale is married to the love of her life that she met in high school. She fell in love with him because he was wearing baseball pants. Ten years later they have three perfectly crazy children and a cat named Demon who likes to wake her up at ungodly times in the night. They live in the greatest state in the world, Texas. She writes contemporary and romantic suspense, and has a love for all things romance. You can find Lani in front of her computer writing away in her fictional characters' world...that is until her husband and kids demand sustenance in the form of food and drink.

Printed in Great Britain
by Amazon